PRAISE FOR A

"A story for the ages: A story born long before the time of man and captured by your writer, Christopher Leibig, who seems to be channeling his work from nether places, bringing you tales that promise to keep you up late turning pages!"

—JOHN ELLSWORTH, *USA Today* and Amazon Bestselling author of *The Lawyer*

"In *Almost Damned*, the sequel to *Almost Mortal*, Christopher Leibig continues the tale of criminal defense attorney, Sam Young, with the gift, or curse, of minor psychic abilities. This book is so much more than a legal thriller; a unique approach to the genre. Attorney Young carries out his legal craft in a remarkable world with multiple planes of existence, that of mere mortals, fallen angels and points where the two intersect. The serious crimes involved and the ways in which Young applies his craft to defend mortals, immortals and those fallen from Heaven are ingenious, fascinating, and thought-provoking. You will enter this alternate world on page one, enjoy the ride to the end of the book, and then anxiously await the time when you can join Sam Young on his next adventure."

—JOHN J JESSOP, author of *Murder by Road Trip*, *Pleasuria: Take as Directed* and *Guardian Angel: Indoctrination*

"Not only does Leibig write from his vast personal experience as an attorney, but he also has extensive knowledge of religious literature; the Bible, the Torah, and the noncanonical book of Enoch. In a masterful stroke of genius, he incorporates ancient religious teachings into contemporary lives."

–AUTHORSREADING.COM

Almost Damned
by Christopher Leibig

© Copyright 2021 Christopher Leibig

ISBN 978-1-64663-293-0

This is a work of fiction. The characters are both actual and fictitious. With the exception of verified historical events and persons, all incidents, descriptions, dialogue and opinions expressed are the products of the author's imagination and are not to be construed as real.

Published by

◄ köehlerbooks™

210 60th Street
Virginia Beach, VA 23451
800-435-4811
www.koehlerbooks.com

ALMOST DAMNED

CHRISTOPHER LEIBIG

VIRGINIA BEACH
CAPE CHARLES

Almost Damned Characters
in Order of Appearance

Tawana Hightower—Alleged rape victim.

Lynn Norwood—Assistant Prosecutor in Bennet County, Virginia.

Samson Young—Criminal defense attorney and partner in Young and Griffin in Bennett County, Virginia. Son of Marcela Young a/k/a Fifika Kritalsh.

David Park—Client of Samson Young, accused of raping Tawana Hightower.

Judge O'Grady—Circuit Court Judge in Bennet County, Virginia.

Myra—David Park's wife.

Amelia Griffin—Samson Young's law partner.

Nguyen Jones—Investigator at Young and Griffin.

Clifford Vick—Diplomat turned international business mogul turned wire-fraud defendant.

Igor Alexi—Client of Young and Griffin, accused of capital murder for robbing and killing his ex-wife.

Eliza Johan—Clifford Vick's girlfriend.

Anonymous caller—with a strange accent.

Jonathon Steinberg—Heroin dealer.

Camille Paradisi a/k/a Trinity Kritalsh—Samson Young's Aunt and former client.

Tre Rittenberg—Bennet County defense attorney.

Farah Hussein- Sam's secretary.

Marcela Young a/k/a Fifika Kristalsh- Samson Young's mother.

Samael—mysterious personage.

Bozo—Farah Hussein's probation officer.

Bernie Genoa—Bennet County attorney and Guardian Ad Litem.

Rajniriput Buterab a/k/a "Raj"—Wealthy philanthropist and alleged but un-convicted former Hungarian mobster.

Esau Jacobs—An "Old man from Appalachia".

Delilah—A psychic in southern Virginia.

Lexi Shapiro—Washington Post journalist.

Steve Buterab—Raj's son, Samson's friend, and local businessman.

Barnabus Farley—Sam's friend. Also a former client alleged drug dealer and cigarette smuggler.

Riker Lugnudsky—Client of Young and Griffin, accused of selling marijuana.

Gus—Assistant Prosecutor in Bennet County.

Chadwick Sparf—Deputy Prosecutor in Bennet County.

Misha Balcheck—Friend of Igor's Alexi's ex-wife.

Mr. Nasser - Night manager, Shangri-La Motel.

Father Paul Andrada a/k/a Paul Kritalsh— Priest. Sam's uncle, Marcela Young and Camille Paradisi's brother.

Alifair Andrada—Samson Young's niece, Camille Paradisi's daughter

Anna Buterab—Steve Buteran's cousin, caretaker for Alifair Andrada.

Bernadette - Clerk at Diagnostia Forensic Analysis and friend of Samson Young.

James—Flight attendant.

Dr. Juliana Kim—Former forensic scientist for Bennet County, current biology professor at the University of Miami.

Dr. William Pitts—Dr. Kim's boyfriend and Neurologist at the University of Miami.

Jimmie Buterab—Steve Buterab's nephew.

Moira—Farah Hussein's roommate.

Anthony Yukov—Igor Alexi's cousin.

Chief O'Malley—Police Chief of Bennet County.

Judge Chan—Circuit Court Judge in Bennet County.

Salome Ortiz—Tunisian/German student killed by Marcela Young in 1957.

Alifair Roja—died and buried in Bennet County in 2000.

Victorio—Camille and Marcela's stepfather's friend.

Miguel Bilbao—Camille and Marcela's stepfather.

Sarah—Bartender at Harpoon Hannah's Bar in Bennet County.

Ms. Dworkin—Riker Lugnudsky's Sixth Grade teacher.

Melvin—Former Law Clerk for Samson Young, current Law Clerk at the Second Circuit Court of Appeals.

Johannes Van Zyl—Man from South Africa who met Camille, Marcela and Paul when they were escaping from Argentina in 1957.

Gabriel, Michael, Uriel, Raphael, Raguel and Sarakiel—Archangels. Members of God's Council.

Azazel—Fallen Angel from the Book of Enoch and Leviticus.

Cinderella Baptista—Camille, Marcela, and Paul's mother.

Zebulon Lucas—man allegedly murdered by Camille in Almost Mortal. Also known as the Rossyln Ripper.

Do not neglect to show hospitality to strangers,
for by this some have entertained Angels unawares.

Hebrews 13:2

PROLOGUE

Samson Young gazed across the Plaza Vieja. He had been sitting at the table alone for precisely three hours. Three elderly women, evenly spaced, walked slowly across the square through a foraging flock of pigeons. He had never met or seen any of the trio before, but he instinctively knew that all three were widows who had been close friends since childhood. Three women. Three hours. Three days. Always in threes. *I have finally become insane.*

Sam looked down at his tablet. His finger hovered over the link that would show him the video clip of his client and, he understood now, his aunt, Camille Paradisi, being shot to death in front of the Bennet County Courthouse three days before. He had seen her brains come out of her head. What he was trying to understand was whether it was indeed possible that she somehow still lived.

Sam watched the clip. He agreed with the general consensus. People survive being shot in the head, but not like that. As the clip ended, he looked up and saw three different women walking towards him, through the pigeons, across the plaza. Camille was one of them. Another was his deceased mother. He had known his mom as Marcela Young. Now he realized the journal was true. Her real name was Fifika Kritalsh. And while she and Camille looked hardly a day over thirty, they were both, in fact, over seventy. And the old woman walking between the two sisters would be their mother, who had died—at least, the first time— back in the fifties. Sam thought back to the journal.

"You mean Job sued God, like in court?"

"Sort of like that."

"Did he win?"

"Of course not."

"The biggest case ever, dude," Barnabas had said.

Finally insane.

CHAPTER ONE

DAY 1, WEDNESDAY, OCTOBER 2, 2019

Alleged rape victim Tawana Hightower had been on the witness stand for only a few minutes, but the prosecutor was already irritated. Tawana wouldn't answer questions directly and used poor English. Tawana's appearance didn't endear her to the prosecutor, either. She looked exhausted, with heavy bags under her eyes staring blankly into the abyss.

"Miss Hightower, please tell us what happened next?" Prosecutor Lynn Norwood pressed.

There's an old practice in criminal trials. When a victim is telling a story to the jury, don't interfere. Every once in a while, just ask, 'What happened next?' Let the witness do the work. But Samson Young, the defense attorney, thought it was a pretty lazy strategy for Norwood to employ with a witness like this. What could go wrong?

Sam Young's attention wandered the courtroom while he listened to Norwood awkwardly attempting to get Tawana to accuse his client of rape—even if only to repeat what she had told detectives months earlier. Sam's mind jumped from the judge to the gallery, to the prosecutor, to his client, to the jury, and back to each again. And it settled finally on Hightower, the internet hooker who had invited Sam's client to the Shangri-La Motel for sex, only to pick up the phone and report a rape as soon as he left.

Sam took a deep breath and studied his client, David Park. David's slumped posture and downcast eyes telegraphed a message ridden with shame. He was a married man with kids and no previous criminal record. Now his habit of hiring prostitutes was being thrown down in public. He might avoid prison and perhaps his marriage would survive. But David's reputation had been destroyed.

Sam knew that David, somewhere inside himself, had been prepared to deal with getting caught for his indiscretions. But rape? Never. If he got caught, he would apologize. Minimize it. Plead for forgiveness. Maybe even buy his way out of it.

Tawana leaned back on the witness stand, rubbed one of her eyes and cleared her throat.

Part of Norwood's obvious frustration with her may have stemmed from what she had chosen to wear to court. In a hooker-rape trial, a plunging neckline said something. And it was hard to say which side it helped. Looking into her eyes from across the well, Sam saw past Tawana's fatigue. It dawned on him that her aw-shucks, beat-down, trashy-hooker routine was a charade, but he had no idea what she had to hide. Somewhere under that rough exterior, a mystery lurked.

"Ms. Hightower," Norwood said, "you texted with the defendant about meeting for sex at the motel. You've shown the jury your escort advertisement. You planned to have sex with the defendant for money. He came to room 2020 at the Shangri-La

Motel. Your room. When he left, you reported that he raped you. What happened after he got there?"

As the prosecutor, Norwood needed to be the first lawyer to demand from her own witnesses the answer to such an obvious question: how did a prearranged, consensual tryst become a rape?

Norwood's frustration suggested she held her own witness in less than perfect regard. Sam glanced at the jury and sensed its disapproval of Norwood's tone. They simply did not like the prosecutor. Two women in the back row seemed, from their disapproving expressions, to especially disdain her. But why? Always so interesting, what people find compelling. One could make the assumption that Lynn Norwood, an attractive, successful young woman, would be the ideal daughter, date, or friend for most anyone in the DC suburbs. What's not to like? But no, this jury was compelled by the hooker and repelled by Norwood. Sam's law partner, Amelia, had once explained jurors' heartfelt and often unpredictable opinions this way: "Everybody has their story. The judge, the prosecutor, the cops, and the pimps and whores, and the do-gooders on the jury. They all have their story and don't figure on anyone finding out about it."

During jury selection, lawyers for both sides discover whether a juror has a criminal record. Felons cannot serve. Often, prosecutors and judges weed out jurors with even petty arrest records.

As a criminal defense lawyer, Sam often marveled at prosecutors' assumptions that jurors lacked seedy secrets and dark urges (realized or unfulfilled) just because they had no criminal record, dressed conservatively, or had a decent job. That is, prosecutors wrongly assumed jurors were as judgmental and prudish as they were.

Sam glanced past the jurors again, careful not to stare or appear too interested in them. *Everybody is just a few months, years, or decisions away from the Shangri-La Motel. Everybody.*

Tawana darted a look at the judge, then back at Norwood. "He was an Oriental," Tawana said. She turned slowly, looked up at Judge O'Grady again, and flinched, like she expected a blow. "Sorry, I know I'm not supposed to say that word. I mean he was a foreigner."

Norwood interrupted Tawana's answer by extending her open palm. "What happened next?"

"I told him I changed my mind," Tawana said. "That I didn't want the date with him." She paused. "I didn't know he'd be a foreigner."

"What happened next?" Norwood asked.

Tawana stared straight ahead.

Norwood took a deep breath at the podium, looked down at her notes, and plowed ahead. "Please continue."

"He pulled out his cock. The next thing I knew, he was stickin' it to me on the bed."

"Ms. Hightower, will you please use more professional terminology," Norwood admonished her as if she were a child.

"Sorry, ma'am. The next thing I knew he pulled out his cock and was having sexual relations with me on the bed."

Norwood sighed again, and too loudly. "What happened next?"

Tawana looked around the courtroom. For the first time, her gaze halted at Sam. "He pretty much nutted all over the place."

This time, a smile softened Norwood's plastic veneer. "Do you mean to say he ejaculated?"

"Yeah, he nutted."

"All right, I think it's time for our lunch break," Judge O'Grady said.

David looked expectantly at Sam as the judge left the bench.

"Relax," Sam whispered. "They haven't heard your side yet. She's hardly even describing a rape. You should have lunch with your wife. I'll see you back here."

Sam watched David and Myra, his wife, leave the courtroom. Sam could tell Myra believed her husband hadn't raped Tawana Hightower. But he couldn't discern what she thought might have actually happened. What occasioned the rape allegation? As Sam had told David when they first met, it wasn't too hard to figure out. If you're gonna hire a hooker, you gotta pay her. The full, agreed-upon price and any suggested tip. What could go wrong?

Sam leaned against the wall in the hallway. Norwood, the detective from the case, and the few courtroom spectators—all staff and law students from the prosecutor's office—disappeared down the long corridor toward the elevators, their lunches, their emails, and their opportunity to discuss Tawana's testimony in her absence. To release some tension, they might make fun of Tawana, the victim for whom they were supposedly advocating. Meanwhile, Tawana sat alone on the bench outside the courtroom. She held her hands in her lap. No friends. No family. No purse. And apparently, no lunch.

Sam heard the courtroom lock from the inside, leaving him and Tawana alone in the silence. Her rubbed his hands over his shaved head then glanced sideways towards her. After a moment, her eyes rested on his. He noticed for the first time how attractive she actually was. She looked two decades younger than her reported age of forty-seven. She wore long, elegant braids. And her hands, which she was previously wringing, now lay still in her lap. Her eyes, blank and tired in the courtroom, were calm and curious.

Then he saw it. *Ha.*

"Aren't you kind of slumming it?" he said.

Tawana narrowed her eyes. "Everybody has their story. How old are you now, Bubba? You forty yet? I always think of you as a teenager. It's been a while."

"We've never met, Tawana."

Tawana narrowed her eyes at him. "Says you."

Sam walked towards her. "You people always have to be mischievous about things, huh? Just calling me would be too normal?"

"Sad to say, Bubba, that the opportune time has finally arrived. And sometimes there's a method to the madness. But first things first. Your Asian does owe me two hundred bucks."

Sam pulled out his wallet. "I've got sixty. And why are you calling me Bubba?"

"Put it towards costs."

"Costs for what?"

"The fee for cancelling the silly ski trip."

"What ski trip? I don't have a ski trip booked."

"Oh, it's as good as booked. And you're running out of time to cancel it. You're way outside your lane, Samson. You gotta put things into perspective."

Sam and Tawana reached the elevators and stood together in the empty hallway for a long moment.

Sam reached into his briefcase, tore a page from a pad, and handed it to her along with a pen. "I need your phone number. The one you really answer." Tawana rested the paper on her palm. He watched her write the number, her long, elegant fingers and red-polished fingernails taking their time with the task.

Sam's phone buzzed. "What's up, Amelia?"

"I've got a problem with a client at the jail. Riker Lugnudsky. One of my appointed cases. Pot distribution. Guy won't talk."

"So what? Not everyone needs to be a snitch."

"I mean he won't speak at all. Just sits there in complete silence."

"Is he batty?"

"Doesn't seem like it. No mental health history that I can find. I think he just won't talk. I've visited him twice, and he sits there saying nothing. He's got court Friday. Any ideas?"

"Let's meet over there this afternoon. Two work?"

"What about your rape trial?"

Sam met Tawana's eyes and pushed the elevator button. "It's gonna end early."

Once in the elevator with Tawana, Sam hit floor three and floor one.

"You've gotta talk to Norwood. About dropping the case. I'm quite sure you can persuade her. But I can't help asking: did David force you or not?"

Tawana looked up at the elevator ceiling as if to ponder the question, or more probably as if to decide whether to answer it. "You can't see it?"

"Really, I can't," Sam said. "I've been alone for four years. Not alone. But I mean, *alone*. The problem is, I see it both ways. Which in a way is—"

"No better than not seeing it at all. Hmm. Well, whether he's guilty or not, it hardly matters now."

The elevator door opened, but Tawana turned around on her way out and held it. After a moment of silence, she let it go, but Sam's hand stopped it as it began to slide shut.

"You know, Bubba, people should stay with their kind."

"You show up as the victim in one of my cases, and now you want to give me cryptic advice?"

"You know what it means."

Sam removed his hand as Tawana turned to walk towards the prosecutor's office. He placed the sheet of paper with Tawana's phone number on it, along with the pen she had used, into a Ziploc bag as the elevator descended.

CHAPTER TWO

"IT'S HARD TO SAY what's bigger, her ego or her tits." Investigator Nguyen Jones leaned over his computer, reading aloud to Sam.

"And you had become so professional lately," Sam said. "Are you watching porn again? Or does this actually have something to do with one of our cases?"

"Everything to do with a case. This is a text message sent last week on Signal, an encrypted phone application."

Sam walked behind Nguyen's desk and zeroed in on his computer screen. "And?"

"These texts went out from Clifford Vick's phone. The phone's not under his name, but from the previous texts, you can tell he's using it. That's Vick referring to Teresa Mellon—the assistant US attorney handling his fraud case—and to her tits."

"How did you get into this?"

"I'm telling you, Bubba, I'm battier than Bruce Wayne when it comes to this stuff. I hacked Vick's Signal account. I'm also onto a private federal law enforcement site. My handle is Spudmuncher101. Believe it or not, *Spudmuncher* was taken. They think I'm an Irish cop, and—"

"Got it." Sam often cut Nguyen off during such digressions. "And when did you start calling me Bubba?"

"Just now." Nguyen continued to punch keys as he focused on the screen.

Sam unfolded his arms and looked out Nguyen's window across the courthouse square. Nguyen's hands glided over his keyboard. Nguyen, in his mid-thirties, looked the part of young computer geek—all business, and all about the tech. The reality was often a bit different.

"I'm about to shave Vick's muskrat."

"Show me what you've got," Sam said.

"Now that I'm into a lot of the social media he uses—under false names—I got this."

Nguyen pulled up a photograph of Clifford Vick, a jailhouse informant—*a snitch*—who the prosecution would be calling against their client in the capital murder trial due to begin in six days. Vick, a diplomat turned international business mogul, having been arrested for a wire-fraud charge in federal court, had spent two days in a cell at the Bennet County Jail last year with Igor Alexi—Sam, Amelia, and Nguyen's client—before being released on bail. All of that was perfectly normal. Short-term cellmates, different courts, different charges, different worlds. The glitch was that Vick, to curry favor with the prosecutors in his own case, was prepared to testify about a conversation he'd had with Igor immediately before his own release. According to police reports, Igor told Vick he not only killed his wife and took her diamond engagement ring, but also "would have screwed the *shluha* if he'd had a *preservatif*." Vick said Igor had used his native Russian terms for *whore* and *condom,* a fact Igor's prosecutors would admit was a fortuitous revelation, since Vick, a one-time international gas trader, knew some Russian, especially of that idiom.

"That's Vick for sure, and his girlfriend. And it looks recent. Mexico maybe?" Nguyen said.

"Belize, fall of 2018," Sam said.

"All right, explain."

Like Amelia Griffin, Sam's law partner, Nguyen often asked Sam to explain how he knew certain obscure pieces of information. It seemed to Sam they did not so much doubt him as enjoy watching him scramble for logical explanations.

"So, check it out; that style of Ray-Bans didn't come out until 2017. The timestamp on the photo says five-thirty p.m., no date. But between May and September, the sun's not going to be that close to setting at five-thirty anywhere tropical. Vick had prostate surgery in March, right? After he started snitching? Also, you can see," Sam pointed to the screen, "that painted bird on the restaurant logo on this thatched roof is the keel-billed toucan, the national bird of Belize. It's gotta be the fall of 2018. Possibly December. Those places always have some sort of Christmas décor that time of year."

"I know the part about the sunglasses is crap. You buy yours at Walgreens. Is the rest true?"

"Only the part about it being Belize in the fall of 2018."

"So, what do you think?" Nguyen asked.

"I get it. Cliff's pretrial supervision order forbids him from leaving the country. And he should not be using aliases for social media, banking, or any other reason while under a federal fraud indictment. I'm glad you got me to ask him about social media when he testified. What a liar. Good stuff. What else?"

"To get to Belize, he's gotta have a fake passport, or at least some way to travel without one; the feds have his. And he's barred from leaving the DC metro area. How do people think they're going to get away with this shit?"

"Because they've been getting away with it for so long," Sam said.

"We're gonna bust up Vick's chiffarobe. Get this." Nguyen clicked open a new file. A page of text messages appeared on the screen, and Nguyen enlarged one of them.

"That's WhatsApp, right?" Sam asked. "An encrypted app. How did you get this?"

"These texts are from Eliza Johan's cell phone—that's Vick's girlfriend. The one in the photo. In this section here—obviously that's Cliff—you can tell from the context that he's talking about his federal case. He even mentions our guy." Nguyen highlighted a portion of the text. "See, here he says, 'Thanks to our friend Boris.' That's a reference—"

"I get it, the Russian," Sam said. "Igor is Ukrainian, but whatever."

"The number Cliff is texting from is assigned by Verizon to a Jonathon Steinberg in Bennet County. But look." Nguyen clicked open another file. "Here's a text thread from the Steinberg phone. There are similar threads every few weeks right up until last month."

"Coded language?"

"Of course." Nguyen quickly highlighted another passage. "Steinberg's talking about heroin. He's communicating with customers. You know—"

"Got it," Sam said.

"Cliff Vick, a critical witness against our capital murder client, has been violating his bond conditions, gallivanting around the world, and even conspiring to sell drugs—opioids, no less—to keep his cash flow going. Not to mention using racist slurs against our client," Nguyen said.

"He's got a lifestyle to maintain," Sam said. "Really, how do you get this stuff without a subpoena?"

Nguyen, as usual when asked about such matters, did not answer. "And now, we've got him creeping on the prosecutor's rack—a woman, mind you, who is getting him a reduced sentence for testifying against Igor. Keep that in mind during jury selection. People are going to hate this guy. Especially women."

Sam's phone buzzed. He walked out of Nguyen's office into his own, and onto the balcony.

"This is Young."

"Samson Young?"

"Yes."

"Samson Young, the attorney who represents Camille Paradisi?"

"I used to—who's this?"

"I believe you still do represent Ms. Paradisi, along with a few others. Am I right?"

"Ms. Paradisi's case was dismissed four years ago. After she was killed. Can I help you?"

The man on the phone began to speak. *Eastern European accent?* Sam listened for several minutes. While he did, his eyes roamed across the courtyard of the Bennet County Court complex. A younger defense lawyer he knew—Tre Rittenberg—exited the courthouse, walking fast. Nervous. Disappointed with a court ruling. The young lawyer slowed and looked across the courtyard at Sam as if sensing he was being watched. They waved at each other. Sam pushed his mind towards the guy. A soft push. *Don't worry, Tre. You had no chance on that issue anyway. Good try.*

As the man on the phone continued talking, Sam realized he had been wrong about the accent. *Not Eastern Europe. But where?* He had one of those voices that was soft to the ears but firm to the mind. Like the voice of someone accustomed to rooms going quiet when he spoke. Sam studied a small photo he had taped onto his desk almost four years ago, when Young and

Griffin had rented the office across from the courthouse. The photograph of him and his mother at his high school graduation, the last photograph of them together.

"Mount Hermon in Israel?" Sam said. "Who are you?"

"I believe you received my package."

"What package?"

"The Mount Hermon Ski Resort package."

Sam watched Tre walk down the street below his window, a bit more bounce in his stride now. He quietly rifled through the inbox on the corner of his desk where Farah, Sam's secretary, stacked non-pertinent items. He held up, then opened, the white envelope that contained a large travel brochure. Mount Hermon Recreational Area.

"I guess I did."

"The opportune venue, no?" the man said.

"I see your point, but what's the venue do for me? And who is this?"

"You're the attorney. And your clients, including Camille Paradisi and your mother Fifika Kritalsh, are very much alive as you well know. Since you've agreed to represent them in this matter, I thought my venue idea would be helpful. I'm on your side. Samael will likely be your opponent. Be careful. He's like catching hold of wind. Don't trust that you know the meaning of anything he says."

"He's dishonest?"

"Not exactly. He just loves, let's say, to thwart simplicity."

A long silence this time. It was a strategy of Sam's. Long silences. To get the other person to speak more. But this guy was using the strategy on him.

"You people are funny with your mysteries," Sam said. "Always so cryptic."

"It's a process, counselor. And besides—" The man paused.

"Let me guess—you're not people."

"You now have your venue. Institution of the lawsuit is your job. What do you call it? Service of process? It's been done before. But I do urge you to be careful."

"Of what?"

"Just be aware. Beginning very soon, I think we're in for a fast-paced conclusion to a troublesome conflict, and such things are always unpredictable. But the opportune time has arrived. I'll see you soon enough. Thanks."

Click. And the man with the accent was gone. Sam flipped through the brochure and then reached into his briefcase. He tugged a plastic glove on, swabbed the envelope seal with one swab and the spine of the Mount Hermon brochure with another, and gently placed the swabs in separate clear plastic bags and sealed them.

"Looks like we're going skiing," Sam said to Nguyen as he walked back into his investigator's office.

"It's October, Bubba."

"To a ski resort, anyway. Mount Hermon Ski Resort."

"Why?"

"You don't want to know."

"So, I gotta ask, you just took a quick call and then categorically stated that we're going skiing on some mountain I've never heard of. Other times, someone asks you to do something that seems rational and you ignore it completely."

Nguyen's attention remained on his computer. "Vick is dead meat. We're gonna roast his chestnuts over an open fire."

"I don't know," Sam said. "Sometimes you get a feeling about who to listen to and go with it."

"Then we're gonna knock the wheels off his chuck wagon," Nguyen said.

"Good one."

• • •

Sam went back to his office, sat, and looked at that day's date, electronically depicted at the bottom right corner of his computer display. It had been more than four years since Camille Paradisi was killed. Since he found out his mother was still alive. Sam had felt each anniversary of the shooting creep up on him, only to pass and collapse back into the frenzy of his busy practice. The date was like a soft deadline that seems so far away until it arrives, yet even then sparks no activity. But suddenly, today, Tawana. And then the phone call.

Farah entered his office. "Sam, I'm gonna take off at lunch. It's my last day, and Bozo—"

"I know," Sam said. "Bozo always wants a urine screen on the last day of somebody's probation."

Sam regarded Farah, the young woman who, two years ago, had been crying in his office after her arrest. Bozo was Farah's nickname for her probation officer. Today she was completing eighteen months of probation for possession of Ecstasy. Her case would be dismissed and she was headed to the University of Virginia in two weeks.

"Does Bozo know you'll be going to a better college than he did?"

"The less he knows, the better. Also, we've got five or six emails from that eLocal thing. What do you want me to do with those?"

A marketing agency, eLocal, helped clients and customers find various services, including legal representation. The agency sent leads to attorneys and charged them if they clicked *claim lead*.

"If it looks lucrative, high profile, or for some other reason especially intriguing, hit *claim lead*. If not, hit *decline*. I trust you. I know, it's annoying. Lots of lame leads."

"Have you ever accepted one of the leads?"

"Never."

"Then why do you subscribe to it?"

"Sometimes I don't know why. What else do you have?"

"That lawyer called again. Bernie Genoa—the one you keep ignoring. Amelia said you called him a bottom feeder."

"Would I say something like that?"

"Maybe."

"Bernie's just kind of a weird dude. He wears sneakers to court and carries a backpack, you know what I mean. Honestly, I hardly know what he does."

"Are you going to call him back?"

Sam shrugged. "I guess so."

"Maybe he got busted for weed or something?"

"Bernie? Not likely. Too dorky for weed."

"Finally, I put a letter on your desk from that weird Appalachian guy. Esau Jacobs."

"Thanks, Farah." Mr. Jacobs, a potential client who would not set up an appointment through Farah, had self-identified merely as "an old man from Appalachia with a serious issue to discuss." No return number. *Funny.*

CHAPTER THREE

ALONE IN HIS OFFICE, Sam pulled Esau Jacobs's letter from a plain white envelope on his desk, addressed to him in neat cursive. The letter inside was similarly handwritten on lined paper.

Dear Attorney Samson Young:

"You're not one of those who can easily hide."
That's what your friend Delilah, the psychic, said when I first sat down at her coffee table. I heard about her mind-reading talents around the way. A direct line to the universe. But that's not what brought me to her. What brought me to her was you, and your nun, Paradisi. You see, I knew she would know you.
"When I do a reading, I like to get a name and an age,"
Delilah said next.
And that was a thorny question, my name and age. The book of Ecclesiastes says there ain't nothing new under the sun, but

whatever corn cobber thought that up hadn't heard of me. Let's just say I've had to use a few different names over the years.

Delilah just watched me as I fidgeted with my photograph of Virginia's First Brigade. I've always been a man of action but not much with words, so I finally just handed the photo to Delilah as my mind flashed back across 150 years to the very day I was transferred from Virginia's Second to General Jackson's First. My mother snipped the photo out of the Richmond Times-Dispatch *and gave it to me when I came home for bedrest after being shot in the chest at First Manassas. I never amounted to much as a soldier, though I was a fine shot and could run like a pony (still can), and that's because I could never make it through a battle without getting my ass shot. Anyway, me and the other new recruits lined up on the wet grass for the photo at Harper's Ferry, and the rest is history.*

Sorry for the digression—back to Delilah's trailer. I was just an old man handing a lady a photograph. But to me, the gesture carried more umph than the handshake between Lee and Grant at Appomattox Courthouse. "I'm sorry to drag you into this, Delilah," I told her, "but my name is Esau Jacobs, and I've been alive for 170 years."

I left Delilah's trailer with your name and number. It's the opportune time for me to meet you, Mr. Young. And I really need to meet Camille Paradisi. I'll be in touch. You can bet on that.

Behind the letter was a copy of a *Washington Post* article by Lexi Shapiro from four years ago, "Body of Murdered Serial Killer Disappears."

Behind that was an ancient, wrinkly photograph snipped from a newspaper article, a black-and-white of a Civil War platoon positioned in two rows, one kneeling in front of the other. *April 11, 1862* was inscribed by hand on the back. Finally, a printed color photograph of an old man with long hair and a long white beard. A selfie, it seemed, with woods in the background. The neat cursive at the bottom of photo said, *Me, August 2, 2019.*

Sam stood and looked out the window and across the courtyard again. It was empty now. Tawana, Mount Hermon, and Esau Jacobs's letter on the same day. *The opportune time, indeed.* He held up the wrinkled photograph. The resemblance between the thin young man in the back row of the war photo and Esau's selfie was obvious, but that did not prove much. Sam snapped pictures of both photos with his phone. *Click. Click. Send.*

"What's your story, dude?"

Then Sam buzzed Farah. "Before you split, what's on the calendar for the rest of the week?"

"Supposed to be for your rape case and then trial prep for Igor."

Sam looked again at the front of Esau's envelope while gently reinserting the letter from the man from Appalachia. "Thanks."

"You gonna call Bernie?"

"See you tomorrow, Farah."

Sam clicked through Igor's file on his computer. Police reports, Nguyen's investigation, and the discovery information from the Department of Forensic Science. He logged on to his bank account. He had a private account, separate from the law firm's, that was accessible to his accountant. Most of his client fees went into the business account. But it was the private account he watched grow, thanks to the less straightforward matters occasionally referred to him, directly or indirectly, by Steve Buterab or Barnabus Farley.

Sam left the office and took the stairs, which left him standing on the sidewalk directly across the street from the courthouse. *Slow time. Observe.*

"Sam?"

Bernie Genoa wore his standard uniform: messy hair, blazer, khakis, sneakers, backpack. Just another character from the courthouse Sam got to know superficially over the years. You hear one thing here, one thing there, and form an opinion based on ghosts. Bernie was known as a weird dude.

"Can I talk to you for a few minutes?"

"Is it about Igor Alexi?"

Bernie looked down, then across the street towards the courtyard. Sam remembered noticing his shyness.

"No," Bernie said.

"Tell you what, Bernie. I've got a murder trial Monday. Can it wait 'til after that?"

"No way. Tomorrow." Sam was taken aback by Bernie's uncharacteristic assertiveness.

"How about Friday?"

Bernie's eyes pierced Sam with a sudden ferocity he never would have known the man possessed. "Tomorrow," Bernie said. "Let's face it, you probably think that because I'm involved, this matter isn't very important. But you're wrong. I assure you the opportune time to speak with me is now."

Yikes.

He watched Bernie stomp across the street towards the courthouse parking lot, and Sam started towards his own car. Next to it sat a shiny black Bentley, engine running and driver behind the wheel.

"I thought you hated the courthouse complex," Sam said.

"Yeah, that's no joke, Bubba. This place pulsates with disturbing cosmic energy. And there are too many assholes nearby to suit me."

"Most of the people in that jail don't belong there, Raj. You of all people know that. And since when do you call me Bubba?"

"I was referring to the judges' chambers, not the jail. So, what's wrong, Samson?"

"Why do you think anything's wrong?"

"I don't *think* stuff. I *know.* You're worried about your pal Igor. But not just him. Not at all just him. By the way, I know

Igor. I'm surprised you never asked me about him. I also know you think you're going crazy. But you know what?"

"Please continue," Sam said.

"You shoulda talked to me before about that, too. I saw your mother go through this. But she learned her way through it. And she was alone, Samson, for most of it. You've got way more to go on than she ever did."

"Speaking of my mother, where is she? I bet you know. And where's Camille?'

Raj lit a cigar and stared through his windshield for a moment. "Whatever you decide to do, I'm with you. My advice is not to worry so much. Let things happen, you know what I mean? None of it's your fault. And you gotta let people help you."

As so often with Raj, he didn't answer the question asked.

"So, you know Igor? How?"

"Let's just say people like him find me. They run me off the road, Bubba. You did, didn't you?"

"You sought *me* out."

"Whatever. I got two thoughts for you, though."

"Yeah?"

"Yeah. One, you gotta call Steve. Get some protection for yourself and your people."

"Why?"

"'Cause you gotta be careful. It's dangerous out there, you know? Just call him. Some of these unsavory types you deal with, you know, not that that's your fault, I'm just sayin'.'"

"No one's ever *just sayin'*," Sam said. "What's your second thought?"

"If you're gonna stay with this matter, just treat it like a regular case. Just be a regular guy. Just do what you do."

Sam stared towards the jail that had housed Camille Paradisi four years earlier and Igor Alexi now.

"Are you just a regular guy, Raj?"

"Human, you bet. Regular guy? Never."

"I'll see you, Raj."

"Be careful, Bubba."

• • •

Flower delivery boy Riker Lugnudsky was an easygoing young lumberjack. Early thirties, long hair, a bushy beard, and a strong slab of a body. According to Amelia, he was accused of selling weed along his flower delivery route. He had been caught with almost a pound of pot—felony territory—in the back of the company van, lost his job, and was now locked up because he would not pay his bond or, apparently, open his mouth to say a solitary word.

Now he sat calmly across the table from Sam, Amelia, and Nguyen in an attorney-client room at the Bennet County Detention Center. His eyes focused straight ahead but did not stare. His calm demeanor and the rumpled collar of his jail jumpsuit gave him the appearance of one who had just awakened from a satisfying nap.

"Riker, this is my partner, Sam Young."

Nothing. Not a change in expression, not a sound.

"This is our investigator, Nguyen Jones. If you talk to us, we can figure out how to help you. Maybe even get you out of here, like tomorrow. It's a felony case, but it's just weed, and you have no record."

Riker's eyes glanced towards Nguyen and back to Amelia. He shifted in his seat a little. But no words. Sam nodded at Nguyen who held a folder of Riker's jail records in his lap. Nguyen leaned towards Riker.

"Somebody put a hundred bucks on your jail commissary, and you haven't spent a cent of it in a two weeks. No extra food, no extra clothes, a radio? Nothing? What's up? You got some kind of plan?"

Riker's eyes darted to Sam, but nothing. Expressionless. Calm. Undistressed.

"The jail records say you have a tattoo on your bicep that reads, *I don't love it*," Nguyen said. "Don't love what? Your bicep?"

Riker looked at his fingernails.

"I have some tattoos, too." Nguyen leaned ever closer to Riker. "You want to know of what?"

Riker remained stoic, but Sam sensed a minor shift of his mood through a slight shrug.

"I have the grim reaper covering my entire back. And he's takin' a shit."

Not a stir from Riker.

"I also have one of a centipede crawling out of my asshole."

The muscles in Riker's face twitched almost imperceptibly, but certainly not enough to mean anything.

"I have a third one that makes my dick look like a Scud missile. That one hurt."

Maybe a flash of light in Riker's eyes, but still close to nothing.

"Hey, man," Nguyen said, "if you won't help us help you, the prosecutors are gonna weed your garden."

No movement.

"Riker Lugnudsky, huh?" Nguyen said. "You got a sister named Alcatraz?"

Riker looked up at the ceiling, watching it for a moment as if something up there had captured his attention.

"Did the kids at school call you Lug Nut?"

Riker shifted in his seat.

"If you're having us on, just sit there and pretend to be really stoned," Amelia said.

Nice try.

"Will you at least sign these releases so we can get some information about your medical history?" she said.

Riker looked down.

Sam hit the buzzer to alert the jail staff that the visit was over. "All right, Riker, Amelia will see you at court."

Riker reached two fingers into the shirt pocket of his jail jumpsuit, the only pocket, a loose-fitting, easily searched pocket, not useful for much of anything but a pen or maybe a small folded note. The paper said, "Sam Young." The door buzzed open, and Sam took the note and stuffed it into his own pocket without reading it.

Sam, Nguyen, and Amelia stood on the street before walking to their cars.

"Who's the prosecutor?" Sam said.

"Gus," Amelia said.

"Perfect. Tell Gus everything. Riker's a college grad, had a job until this arrest, and must be suffering some kind of mental trauma, which is manifesting in his inability to communicate. Which means he's incompetent to stand trial, and if he remains in jail, he'll be in the Department of Corrections mental hospital for months on a case where he probably deserves probation even if he's guilty. Also, the lab will take six months to test the pot. Basically, this guy needs legit mental-health treatment outside the jail, which he can't get while he's in jail—and he won't pay his bond. It's a major injustice waiting to happen."

"What if Gus tries to solve the problem by changing the bond to personal recognizance? Lets Riker out without paying?" Amelia said.

"Make sure to tell him that won't work. Riker is too catatonic to sign the bond paperwork to get released on his own recognizance. He can't even fill out a jail form to order a cup of soup. Ask Gus to drop the case for now. We'll get him some help, and they can recharge the case once he's competent. Once he can talk, at least."

"Why would Gus do that?"

Sam took a step towards the parking lot. "That's an interesting thing about Gus. He smokes weed and doesn't think it should be illegal. He just needs an excuse to help a guy like Riker. And you should know another thing about Gus."

"What?"

"Once the case is gone, he'll forget, either accidentally or on purpose, to re-charge, even after Riker's voice heals up."

Sam began to walk away, but Amelia touched his arm, raising her eyebrows at him. "Dude, the note."

Sam looked blankly at both of them, suddenly needing a drink badly enough to begin planning his day around it. Like, next stop, 7-Eleven bad. Sam removed the note from his pocket and handed it to her. Before Amelia opened it, he offered, "It says something like, people should stay with their own kind."

Amelia handed the note to Nguyen who glanced at it and handed it back to Sam just as Deputy Commonwealth Attorney Chadwick Sparf hustled into their space. Sparf, who had been about to dismiss the murder case against Camille Paradisi four years ago, before she was murdered, was, for better or worse—more often than not, worse—a regular opponent.

"All right, Young, Amelia, we're less than a week from trial," Sparf said.

He referred to Igor's Monday trial date as if they all were not hyperaware that it was bearing down on them.

"I just had a final meeting with the victim's family," Sparf said. "We talked everything through again, and finally, if your guy is willing to accept responsibility for what he did, I can offer a straight-up plea to first-degree murder, no death penalty, free to argue."

Sparf's offer, if accepted, would not only spare Igor a death sentence, it would also allow him to ask the judge for a sentence of less than life in prison—a result that could never happen after losing a trial. For someone at age forty-one, it meant an actual chance, albeit perhaps a small one, to be free again someday. Amelia glanced at Sam, Nguyen, and then the ground.

"Thanks, Chad," Sam said. "We'll let you know."

Sparf, blinking quickly in the bright sun, snapped his head quickly from one member of the Young and Griffin legal team to the other.

"Excuse me!? You suggested you wanted this deal months ago. That's it? You'll let me know? I just spent all morning getting these people on board, and—"

"I hear you, Chad," Sam said. "We'll get back to you. Things may have evolved."

"Evolved? Are you kidding? Alexi's going down if you have the trial and you know it. We've got DNA, and he confessed. What evolved?"

None of them answered. Sparf turned on his heel. "Deadline tomorrow." He started to trudge back across the courtyard toward his office but spun back around and addressed Nguyen directly. "By the way, Mr. Jones, the Commonwealth does not appreciate the way you treat your subpoenaed witnesses."

Nguyen looked at Sparf, then at Sam.

"Sam, you might like to know that your investigator served a trial subpoena to a Misha Balcheck, a friend of the murder victim, while the man was sitting on the toilet at Starbucks. Mr. Jones balled up the summons, rolled it into the stall, took a photo under the stall door of the man picking it up, and then stated"— Sparf read aloud from his phone—"'You're served, amigo.'"

"He was dodging me," Nguyen said. "And he was a lot more than her friend."

"The proper way to serve a subpoena is introducing oneself accurately, presenting the document to the subpoenaed party by describing its true nature, and stating, 'You are officially served, sir, or ma'am,'" Sparf said with mounting indignation and vitriol. "Do you think invading someone's private space and using racially charged language is an appropriate way to conduct legal business in Bennet County?"

Nguyen's eyes widened. "*Amigo?* Racially charged? It means *friend.* Besides, the guy's Russian."

Sam imagined a cold shot of vodka easing into his stomach. "Appropriate enough," he said.

"Tomorrow," Sparf said, walking away.

"Sorry, Sam," Nguyen said. "The guy was dodging me, and—"

"I've got no problem with it," Sam said. "Next time, just don't tell the prosecutor what you know about a witness. The part about him being more than a friend."

"Sorry."

"He's just mad 'cause you're always stitching up their softballs."

"Not bad," Nguyen said.

"I'll see you guys." Sam turned towards the parking lot.

"Sam, wait," Amelia said. "Are you serious about not trying to get Igor to take the deal? Now you *want* him to go to trial on this case and risk his life? Why?"

"Sometimes I don't know why."

• • •

Half an hour later, Sam parked in front of the Shangri-La Motel, a town relic that had been sitting on the outskirts in far east Bennet County since he was a boy. He stepped out of the Escalade and took the outside staircase and narrow cement walkway to room 220. He leaned back on the rail. He glanced around the mostly empty parking lot and then back down the main road. Quiet. An early summer evening, and the warehouses and storage places were closed. The Shangri-La Motel, built for motorists long before the fancy hotels, shops, and restaurants that made downtown Bennet an extension of Northwest Washington, was now well-known in Bennet County for prostitution and drug activity. So well-known that Sam once heard a vice detective say that merely parking at the Shangri-La amounted to probable cause for an arrest. Sam thought about the mysterious phone call and the man from Appalachia, but put them out of his head. He turned back to the door and focused on it, but softly. *Slow time. Observe.*

"Can I help you?"

Sam turned and faced a Middle Eastern man in jeans and a T-shirt.

"I'm the night manager here. Can I help you? You've been staring at that door for five minutes, but the person renting that room is not home right now."

Sam now saw the man's name tag.

"You looking for someone? Maybe you got the wrong room?"

"Sorry, Mr. Nasser," Sam said. "Maybe she'll be around tomorrow."

"He or she may or may not be here tomorrow, if they're still a guest at that point. I don't mean to run you off. Just asking if you're okay, my friend. You sick or something?"

Nasser, as the night manager of the Shangri-La, was likely not the type to run people off for minor odd behaviors. But neither was he the type to divulge information about his guests.

"I'm okay, Mr. Nasser," Sam said. "Thanks." He walked past Mr. Nasser, across the walkway and down the stairs, then climbed into his Escalade and exited the Shangri-La parking lot. He knew nothing more at all about the alleged rape committed by David Park earlier that year—not that it mattered anymore. But he knew something very new about Tawana Hightower.

CHAPTER FOUR

SAM STOOD ON THE large rooftop patio of his house on Monument Row and looked down at the D-Day Memorial and the DC skyline behind it. A vodka tonic sat on the balcony rail. The huge rowhouse near the Key Bridge had been previously owned by Barnabus Farley who'd gifted it to Sam shortly after Sam's return from Cuba four years earlier—the trip on which he learned, without doubt, that his Aunt Camille and his mother were both still alive. Sam had not actually seen Barnabus since he'd walked away from Sam in the medical examiner's parking lot, the day after Camille died. Barnabus had explained the transaction's details to him in a brief phone call.

"Barnabus, this is crazy. Besides, I can't even afford the taxes on the place."

"Dude, stop being such a pussy. Check your bank account tomorrow. See you soon."

"When, Barnabus? When am I going to see you?"

"You'll see me at the opportune time."

No direct contact from Barnabus since. Just a call from a DC lawyer, some paperwork, and Sam owned 3301 Monument Row. Every so often since then, a legal favor here, some investigation there for various clients referred by Barnabus, and Sam's personal bank account grew.

Sam picked up his drink, sat on one of the sectional couches, and opened his laptop. The heat of the day was lifting as the sun went down, and as always, Sam felt the quiet settle in as the first bit of alcohol hit his stomach. He clicked open two files, neither of which he had looked at it in, what, a year? Two even? One file was a personal timeline he'd created, and the other was constructed by his mother, Marcela Young, as part of her doctoral dissertation.

Creation—4004 BCE
Curse (Adam, Eve, and the Serpent)—4004 BCE
Enoch "Walks with God" (ascends to heaven)—3082 BCE
Global Flood—2348 BCE
Tower of Babel—2242 BCE
Egyptian Civilization—2242 BCE (Genesis 12)
Call of Abraham—1922 BCE
Ice Age Peak—1848 BCE

The standard creationist historical timeline went on through the birth of Christ. The traditionally understood times of Biblical events, important generally only to those who took the Hebrew Bible literally.

You're not one of those who can easily hide. Sam Googled a Bible verse he had first seen in his mother's dissertation four years ago. The Fallen Angels from Mount Hermon. Maybe 3100 BCE?

Genesis 6:1–7: Now it came to pass, when men began to multiply on the face of the Earth, and daughters were born to them, that the sons of God saw the daughters of men, and they were beautiful, and they took wives for themselves of all whom they chose. And the Lord said, "My spirit shall not strive with man forever, for he is indeed flesh; yet his days shall be one hundred and twenty years." There were Nephilim on the Earth in those days, and also afterward, when the sons of God came to the daughters of men and they bore children to them. Those were the mighty men of old, men of renown. And God saw that the wickedness of man was great on the Earth, and that every imagination of the thoughts of his heart was only evil continually.

On his phone, Sam positioned the photo of the young soldier Esau, with his army troop, next to the recent photo of old man Jacobs. He zoomed in on each, one and then the other, repeatedly. While zooming in on the *Times-Dispatch* photograph, he noticed for the first time a small caption that named the soldiers in the photograph in no apparent order. None was named Esau Jacobs.

Sam clicked on his next document, *The Doctoral Dissertation of Marcela O. Young: Jesus, Resurrection, and the Occult,* and scrolled to page thirty-seven:

The use of term "sons of god" in Genesis 6 has been, deliberately or otherwise, misconstrued by theologians since the unitary God concept became important around the time of the Council of Nicaea in 325 CE, well before almost anyone could actually possess, let alone read, the incongruous pieces of historo-mystical lore which became the Bible. But this short verse told an important story. Anywhere the term "sons of God" appeared in the Hebrew Bible meant only one thing—angels. The term was next used in Job 1:6–7:

There was a day when the sons of God came to present themselves before the Lord, and Satan came amongst them. And the Lord said unto Satan, "Whence comest thou?" Then Satan answered the Lord, and said, "From going to and fro in the Earth, and from walking up and down in it."

In this verse God holds a meeting in Heaven with angels and Satan—sons of God. Thus, the term as used in Genesis 6 tells us that at a point in time after creation, and before the Flood, angels descended to Earth, mated with human women who bore offspring. Having been born of defiant, lustful, and corrupted angels, they were themselves evil. Or so it is said.

Sam's phone buzzed.

"What do you got?"

"Oh, man, we're gonna spike this fucker's punchbowl," Nguyen said.

"Whose?"

"Vick's."

"What about Jacobs?"

"Oh. Facial recognition technology is being used by thousands of platforms—Facebook, the feds, your own phone, you name it. It's easy. It detects faces in group photos, matching two faces, finding similar faces, whatever."

"Okay."

"And if the photos are legit, I think our new pal Esau Jacobs could be the poster boy for Viagra if he's still on the dating scene."

Sam looked back at his mother's dissertation, skimming the next passage, imagining her hovering over it alone in her study.

"Which I'm sure you already knew," Nguyen said.

Sam hung up, finished half his drink in one gulp, and leaned forward to pull up another document on his laptop. The sun was down now. He glanced at the stars, dulled by the city lights but visible in the cloudless sky. *SY notes.*

He searched the document and pulled up what he needed. The direct descendants of Adam through the line of his third son, Seth: Adam, Seth, Enos, Canaan, Mahalaleel, Jared, Enoch, Methuselah, Lamech, Noah. They were the apocryphal patriarchs of those who later became the Israelites. But it was not the obedient Seth, history's oldest man Methuselah, or the ever-famous Noah, who informed Sam's research, but Enoch—the principal intermediary between two sides of the conflict between the *Fallen Angels* and the *Righteous Angels*. In other words, Sam mused, the first Biblical defense attorney. And maybe the last.

Sam clicked back to the dissertation:

There was no doubt that God viewed the transgressions of the angels, not only mating with the women but also poisoning human minds, as unforgivable:

It happened that after the sons of men had multiplied in those days, that daughters were born to them, and they were beautiful. And when the angels, the sons of God, beheld them, they became enamored of them, saying to each other, "Let us select for ourselves wives from the progeny of men." Their number was two hundred who descended upon Mount Hermon. And the women conceived, bringing forth demons. The angel Azazel taught men to make swords, knives, shields, and breastplates, mirrors, and the use of paint for beautifying the eyebrows. Impiety increased and fornication multiplied. And God said to his loyal angels, "Bind Azazel hand and foot, cast him and the others into darkness. All the Earth has been corrupted by the effects of the teaching of Azazel. To him, therefore, ascribe the whole crime." (Book of I Enoch, 7–10).

Enoch went on to explain how his entreaties in Heaven to forgive the Fallen Angels failed, and how God's most powerful and loyal angels—Raphael, Michael, Gabriel, Sarakiel, and Uriel—played various roles in bringing Azazel and the two hundred Fallen Angels into submission and eventual imprisonment. But the descendants of the Angels, the men of renown spoken of in Genesis, remained. Thus, the need for the Flood, sparing only Noah and his family. The Bible, while failing to mention the names of any of the wives of Noah's sons, did not dodge the glaring omission in God's plan—that one or more of the wives of Shem, Ham, and Japeth could have been the offspring of Fallen Angels.

Sam walked quickly down the spiral staircase and into his kitchen, downed one glass of vodka, and filled another. Early yet. He sat on the couch, turned on the TV, and hit a number on his phone. Sam imagined the tough old priest sitting in front of his television. Like the regular guy he very much was not. But on the other hand, kind of was.

Sam took a long sip from his drink. "Hey, how's our girl?"

"Oh, she's great, Sam. That nanny Anna is something. She makes things easy for me."

"You've been thanking me for that for four years. We're even."

"Anyway, I'd be screwed without her—a man my age can't raise a child."

"Can I come by Friday night? There's some stuff I want to run by you."

"Of course."

"It might be kind of late."

"You? Late?"

An hour later, Sam made another drink and stood at the railing of the rooftop balcony watching the city. Four years ago, Nguyen had ginned up a will for Camille, which mandated that Father Andrada take custody of her child upon her death. Sam thought of his mother's journal, the part about her mother leaving her in Bariloche when she was a young girl:

My mother had come to me the day after she died. She let me touch her, caressed my head, and promised me that no matter what I felt, I was never really alone. I hate that she believed she had to go. To leave me again. But as she put it, resurrected ones should never linger for too long. "Jesus knew that, and so do I." Her promise to always be with me in my heart was not very consoling. As quickly as she had come, she was down the mountain road and out of town. Despite what my mother said, I feel so alone and scared. I wish I were an angel, as I feel my mother may have been. But I worry that I am just crazy. Or even a demon.

Sam's phone's home screen depicted four-year-old Alifair Andrada. She was smiling, standing alone on a sidewalk in front of neatly cut grass, probably somewhere on the grounds of Holy Angels. She was too young to question her situation. To ask why she was being raised by her uncle, and a priest at that. To ask where her father was. Or for more information about how her mother died.

Sam opened a thin manila file. The Virginia Department of Forensic Science's DNA file for the Igor Alexi case. The DNA evidence in the case was harmful but could still be argued either way. After all, Igor's wife had been killed in the home they had, until recently, shared. Naturally, his DNA was all over the place. On the other hand, a well-used light switch would likely carry the DNA profile only of someone who had touched it rather recently, and Igor had told police he had not visited the home for weeks before someone stabbed his wife to death. Yelena Alexi's clothes, stained with her own blood, had no stray genetic markers. But Igor's genetic profile was nevertheless part of the case. Could his genetic markers have remained on the light switch since he was last at the house? Everything in Igor Alexi's case could be argued either way. The certificate of analysis arguably matching his DNA to the genetic sample found on the light switch was accompanied by an inch-thick stack of lab notes supporting its conclusions.

One thing jumped out about Igor Alexi's forensic DNA profile; there was a single genetic marker at each genetic location: one marker, not two. Sam thought back to Juliana's testimony from Camille's furlough motion from four years ago. The day before Camille was killed, he had asked Juliana on the witness stand about how the Zebulon crime scene evidence compared to Camille Paradisi's DNA.

"Is that an incomplete result?"

"Yes. Every human's DNA has a pair of markers at all fifteen of the sixteen Powerplex loci, one from the mother, one from the father. This result is incomplete in that it lacks any markers at six of the loci. It happens sometimes, quite often really, with weak DNA results. When there's not enough DNA on a crime scene item."

"Is it not incomplete in another respect?" Sam asked.

Juliana looked up at the judge as if to stress the importance of this answer. But the answer was for the press.

"I thought so at first," Juliana said. "It's as if she has a mother but no father. For a human being, I consider it categorically impossible."

"But Paradisi exists."

"No doubt."

Now Sam's phone buzzed. A Florida number. Miami. *How Providential.*

"Hey, Juliana, how's the university life? Better than working?"

"Hmm, South Beach. Positively glamorous. Actually, it's hot as shit. My classes are pretty cool, though. And the lab makes Virginia DFS look like the Stone Age."

"So, what do you got on the Alexi profile?"

"Probably a long conversation, but I think you know the basics."

"Let's have it anyway."

"Well. I've only ever seen one other DNA profile like Alexi's, and you know when. I've checked all the raw data, and the chart is accurate. Scientifically, Igor Alexi cannot possibly exist. He's homozygotic at all loci."

"Unfortunately for him, the Commonwealth of Virginia disagrees. They think he's locked up in the Bennet County Jail awaiting trial and, they hope, execution."

"I'll take your word for it," she said. But that mass of flesh posing as a defendant can't exist. He's homozygotic at seventeen loci. It can't happen."

"How is it he got a Y chromosome?"

"That's a good question, Sherlock, but he does. Where's his mother? Can you type her?"

"Maybe. So, you'll testify?"

"At trial? To what? That his weird profile, human or not, is on the light switch? Isn't that the prosecutor's point?"

"No, not at trial."

"What then?"

Sam drained his drink and closed the file.

"Not sure yet, but I envision more of a congressional kind of thing, or a press conference."

"Hmm. What are you up to?"

"Just be ready," Sam said. "You've explained it before. Igor Alexi's DNA can't possibly exist. He can't exist, based on your knowledge of the human genome. In other words, he's not human, at least not completely. Kind of like some other people we know."

"Like maybe a lawyer from Virginia?"

"Ha. Goodbye, Juliana."

"Wait, I called for another reason too."

"Let's have it."

"I started seeing someone."

"Okay. That's good, right?"

"Yeah, it is. I guess I just thought I should tell you."

"Thanks, Juliana. Does that mean I can't visit?"

"Hmm. Don't think so. When?"

Sam shot a text to Farah for her morning to-do list and then punched some keys on his laptop, bringing up his mother's journal.

"Sam, are you there? When?"

"Tomorrow."

• • •

His legs stretched in front of him on his bed, Sam scrolled through his mother's journal for the portion that had jumped into his head.

Moments later I stood by the door, breathing deeply, rhyming my breaths with Marcus's, who still slept soundly with his drunken little snores. "Thank you," I said aloud. As for whether I was thanking Marcus, the universe, or even the Great One, I had no idea. Leaving Marcus alive puts us in danger. He'll wish to chase us, for the money and for me. Then why the inner sense of levity as I softly shut the door on his snoring? I took the stairs, popped out on a side street, and purposefully crossed the street and entered the cathedral. It was near midnight. An old woman knelt in a pew near the front, sobbing. I strolled straight down the center aisle, leaning back on my spine. Slow time. Observe. Christ on the cross looked kind, but his depiction mirrored his reality by remaining still, unmoved by Earthly events. I could feel the tears on my face. I whispered to him. A short message. Part of me wanted to tell the Great One's son I was sorry for everything. For Salome and Ortiz and Miguel, and the tan-coat soldiers, and the hophead, and the drug dealing, and for selling my body, and for all my other sins. But all my life I have only acted consistently with my nature. I may as well be what the universe says I am. I am anyway. And yet, why did I leave Marcus alive? I wanted to ask Jesus. But instead, I said something more important.

"You made me this way. You get that part, right?"

And like always with the Great One and his Son, nothing.

Sam pulled up a blank Word document and began to type.

You are commanded to appear.

His phone buzzed, but he ignored it, staring at the computer screen, hands frozen with indecision above the keyboard.

You are commanded to appear.

Sam set the laptop aside, picked up his phone, and scrolled through it. He set his alarm just as a new email hit. From eLocal. The lame client leads were usually people charged with DWI or other relatively minor cases. Sam often opened them anyway, skimmed the lead, and always hit *decline lead* right away so the opportunity could go to another attorney. Sam clicked on it.

You and your friends are all going to fucking die.

He took a screenshot and clicked *claim lead.*

He lay back on the bed and looked at his phone, zooming in again on the smiling Alifair. Maybe *she* would turn out normal. Sam looked deeply into her eyes—one brown, one green—and then drifted off.

And I went with the Holy Angels to another place. And there were seven splendid mountains, each different from the others. And three mountains were in the east, and strengthened by being placed one upon the other, and three were towards the south, strengthened in a similar manner. There were likewise deep valleys. And the seventh mountain was in the midst of them. In length they all resembled the seat of a throne. And Raphael said to me, "Your plea shall be heard here by God's Council."

Sam awoke to his buzzing phone. It was just after six and Amelia was making sure he was awake. A morning ritual. He clicked decline, texted *on it, thanks* to Amelia, and looked around the room. He knew his dream had been from the book of Enoch, though a passage he had never read. Enoch's narrative of visiting heaven.

His laptop still sat next to him on the bed. He touched a key and brought the screen to life. The Word document from the night before was still queued up, but now complete.

Summons

You are hereby commanded to appear at noon on October 9, 2019, at the summit of Mount Hermon in the land of Canaan to answer to the below-described suit in equity, to wit, to show cause why (1) Azazel and the Elohim, the Angels who descended onto Mount Hermon, having been convicted and sentenced to seventy generations in fire for their crimes against God and humanity, should not forthwith be returned to Heaven given the expiration of such sentences; and (2) the souls of mixed descent, the blameless offspring of the above-described Angels, should not forthwith join the human race. Both causes of action rely upon the need to avoid unwarranted disparities between God's treatment of the various transgressors against God's law, and the egalitarian principles set forth below, taken together and in combination with each other and related rules and dictates, which, taken together and in combination with each other, operate to invalidate any and all previously made pronouncements concerning forgiveness, arbitrary punishments, and punishment of descendants for transgressions of their forbears:

Do to others whatever you would have them do to you. This is the essence of all that is taught in the law and the prophets. (Matthew 7:12, also known as the Golden Rule)

Fathers shall not be put to death because of their children, nor shall children be put to death because of their fathers. (Deuteronomy 24:16)

Fathers shall not be put to death because of their children, nor shall children be put to death because of their fathers. But each one shall die for his own sin.
(2 Kings 14:6)

The son shall not suffer for the iniquity of the father, nor the father suffer for the iniquity of the son.
(Ezekiel 18:20; cf. Jeremiah 31:30)

The Lord, a God merciful and gracious, slow to anger, and abounding in steadfast love and faithfulness, keeping steadfast love for thousands, forgiving iniquity and transgression and sin. (Exodus 34:6–7)

Failure to appear to answer this suit in equity shall be taken as a default of any position contrary to this suit in equity, and shall result forthwith in the open and worldwide declaration of public proof of the existence on Earth of the aggrieved parties and of the wrongs suffered by them.

Sam clicked "save."

CHAPTER FIVE

DAY 2, THURSDAY, OCTOBER 3, 2019

As on almost every morning for the last four years, Sam walked into the expansive bathroom adjoining his bedroom. The long, double-sink vanity was empty but for a small collection of bathroom supplies crowding the corner.

Standing in front of the mirror, Sam hit a number on his phone.

"Hey, Sam. I booked your ticket and hotel. Kinda random, though—don't you have a murder trial Monday?"

"In that vein, Farah, Nguyen's busy today, so I need you to serve a subpoena for Igor's case."

"Oh. As long as you tell me how."

"Nguyen prepped the subpoena, and it's in a file on the right corner of his desk."

"Got it," she said. Sam imagined her swooping into his office, phone crooked in her neck, opening the file.

"You see the name. Jonathon Steinberg. He's a concierge at the Residence Inn by the bridge, and he's working today. Nguyen has his photo in the file. You drive down there and hang out in the lobby until you see him, and then you politely walk up and hand it to him. Then you say, 'You've been served, sir.' Then you walk away and fill in the second sheet, which confirms that you served him and the time, and you put that back in the file. Oh, and he's not going to be happy, so walk away fast."

"I have to do it when he's at work?"

"Best at work. He can't freak out."

"What if he doesn't take it?"

"He will, believe me. A concierge is going to take hold of a sheet of paper handed to him by a young woman in a hotel lobby. But if he doesn't take it, then touch him lightly with it, and say the same thing. That counts, even if it winds up on the floor. As long as he sees it. Then walk away."

"What's he got to do with Igor?"

"You don't need to know. But basically, he sells drugs for Vick."

Sam looked at himself closely in the mirror, another daily ritual. *How hungover am I?*

He scrolled through his phone, looking for the eLocal message from the night before. The message, as well as his screenshot of it, was gone.

He hit a number on his phone.

"Hey, brother, wow, what an honor! An actual phone call from Samson Young himself."

"That's BS, Steve."

"Yeah, yeah, whatever. You calling to offer me kickbacks on my referrals, huh? You must be rich enough by now, bro."

"I can't do kickbacks, but your help is always appreciated. I can hire you back, though."

"Yeah, yeah, I get it. A no-show job. You gotta cover your tracks."

"No, I mean it. I need your services."

"Of course you do. Is my cousin still doin' okay over at the church, with the kid? The priest?"

"Anna's still doing great, I hear."

"That's good. She needs to learn some skills so I can get her married off. She also needs to lose some weight. I thought maybe chasin' that kid around would help. But so far, no offers."

Typical Steve Buterab. Gifting those in his orbit with protection and money, but at a paternalistic and condescending cost. Steve's cousin Anna, in her early twenties, had readily agreed four years earlier to move into Father Andrada's residence at Holy Angels and become the caregiver for Camille's daughter, Sam's cousin, Alifair Andrada. Sam had always believed the nanny opportunity was a much-appreciated ticket for Anna to be less dependent on Uncle Steve and the rest of the Buterab family. Sam paid her well, and she well knew it was unnecessary to keep Uncle Steve fully informed about her compensation package.

"I want protection for my partners," Sam said.

"Yeah, my dad said something about that," Steve said. "You want someone on Amelia and what's his name, the weird investigator dude?"

"Exactly."

"Follow them and camp out at homes and the office? That's expensive, buddy. But I guess you know that."

"Indeed. Starting, like, now. I'm running late for work, then I'm off to the airport. I'll leave this to you."

"I'm on it. I've got just the guys in mind. But what about you, comrade? You bulletproof now?"

"Maybe."

"So, I gotta ask. Who exactly are we worried about?"

"Can't say. Maybe I'm just overly paranoid."

"Ain't no such thing, pal. I got you covered."

"Thanks, Steve."

"You're welcome, Bubba."

Sam stared deep into his own eyes in the mirror. One brown, one green.

• • •

"Sam! Long time no see."

Bernadette, the clerk at Diagnostia, smiled at him as he leaned against the counter.

"My girlfriend, you know, she'd been behaving herself. Until recently, that is."

"Oh, that's too bad. What do you got?"

"A pen, a sheet of paper, like a note, and two envelopes."

"That slut's been busy, huh?"

"If you only knew."

"You're crazy, Sam. You know the police chief asked me to report to him about any results you ask for?"

"But you don't, do you?"

"Expedited results as usual?"

"Extra expedited."

"How extra?"

"Your website says you can get presumptive paternity results in ninety minutes."

"That costs."

Sam held up his credit card. "Twenty-five hundred, six hours. I know you can do it. Just a prelim result. Just typing charts. And please email the results to me, and to this email address, too."

Sam handed her Juliana's business card and five Ziploc bags, one each for the note from Riker Lugnudsky, the paper and the pen touched by Tawana, and the envelopes from the man from Appalachia and the mystery caller.

"There will likely be stray profiles on some of them," Sam said, "including mine. But let's see what we can get."

"You know, Sam, I've got to tell you that—"

"In my heart I already know."

• • •

"May I offer you a preflight beverage, sir?"

The male flight attendant placed a napkin on Sam's tray table. He was one of only four passengers in first class, an extravagance he allowed himself when a client seemed not to care about costs.

"Tito's and tonic, and make it a triple," Sam said.

The young man smiled. "Mr. Young, we are limited to two servings per passenger, per order."

Sam nodded, opening his laptop. "All good."

He opened a fresh Word document, then a web browser, and glanced out the window. Two airport officials were speaking to each other, both looking at the plane every moment or so. He relaxed his mind.

"Here you go, Mr. Young."

The flight attendant was back with a large cup of ice, a can of tonic, and three small bottles of vodka. "Enjoy."

"Thanks, James."

James winked at him. "You got it, Bubba."

Sam dumped the first bottle into the ice cup and drank it in one gulp as James moved to the next passenger. Sam sipped the next vodka and focused on his laptop.

"Here you go, Mr. Young." James slipped two more small vodka bottles into Sam's seat pouch.

"You rock, James."

Sam opened a document.

Story of Samael:

Samael is an archangel in Talmudic stories as well as Christian tradition and demonology. Other religions also believe in stories of Samael. Samael is often thought to be both good and evil. It is said he is God's main representative on Earth. Samael is likened to or even conflated with Satan because he is usually tasked with morbid assignments, often playing the role of a mischievous and scheming investigator. He has appeared as a man and a woman, or even as various animals—like the snake in the Garden of Eden. He is sometimes considered the chief of the evil spirits, other times only one of many. He is a Fallen Angel from the original rebellion against God but remains one of God's servants.

Sam finished the vodka. He leaned back and shut his eyes.

"Mr. Young? Mr. Young? We're landing in Miami. Thought you may want this." James held out a bottle of water.

"Thanks, James."

CHAPTER SIX

AFTER A VISIT TO the business center, Sam sat at the Hilton bar in front of a cold martini.

"Hey there," Juliana said. They embraced, and Juliana and a gray-haired gentlemen took seats next to Sam.

"William Pitts," the man said, gripping Sam's hand warmly. "Pleasure to finally meet you."

"Likewise."

"I wanted you guys to meet, but also, William works with me at U of M and is, in fact, a neurologist with an interest in neurochemistry. He's interested in your . . . project. And I just got your Diagnostia results. That was fast. I hope you don't mind that I shared our, you know, discoveries with him. He is *really* smart."

Sam regarded William, an earnest professor type who was obviously really into Juliana. He smiled at the compliment, which he had not seen coming.

"Well, that's probably what we need. You trust him, I trust him. Welcome to the Black Mirror, William."

Juliana took a folder out of a backpack and opened it on the bar.

"First off," William said, "as I'm sure you know, this is fascinating stuff. We could get famous with these profiles. You give me permission, I'd do a paper on this, which, I understand, is the kind of thing you may want. Also, it may interest you that I went to divinity school way back when. And I understand that there may be some, I guess, religious implications at play. But let's start with science."

"I'm listening."

"What I have here are forensic DNA profiles of Camille Paradisi and Igor Alexi and four other results. Who are they?"

"Result one is a swab from a note from my client, Riker Lugnudsky; two is a swab from two items for a woman named Tawana Hightower. The third and fourth are from envelopes, one maybe from a guy named Esau Jacobs, the other unknown."

"Okay, so first off," Juliana said, "we already know about Paradisi. Alexi, Riker, Tawana, and this guy Esau, if these are complete results, are also homozygotic at all tested loci. Which, I'm guessing, you already suspected. Statistically, as you know, it basically can't happen. Statistics can play with your head, though, so let's just say, as I did in court four years ago, that Paradisi is a regular human who defied the odds, who happened to get the same genetic marker at all of the Powerplex loci. I mean, as odds go, the chances of this happening are remote, in the trillions even if her parents were identical twins, and scientists would normally be willing to call it impossible. But hey, she was alive, and these were government results from a blood draw, so, sure, whatever—it happened. No one is going to make the full buy-in that she's not human. They'll say, yeah, it's weird, and everyone thought the gunshot killed her, but it didn't. Just an odd occurrence—not a miracle."

Sam finished his martini and glanced at his phone. Amelia, texting. *Call me!!* And again, *As soon as you land, call me!!* Sam ordered a glass of wine. One thing at a time.

"Okay," Sam said. "And?"

"And even if people can accept this odd occurrence regarding Paradisi, it defies all logic to believe the same thing could happen to *four* other people that *you* know. Sam, what I am saying is that if these results are all legit, we have discovered a new species, and you have irrefutable proof if it." Juliana looked at William. "Tell him what you want to do."

"Sam, I'd like to get new genetic samples from a couple of these people and get Juliana to map them with a different sort of DNA testing."

"Like what?"

"All you have here is forensic testing. It uses noncoding locations in our genes to identify people, but the locations don't code for characteristics. The locations don't tell us anything about diseases, personality traits, or anything else. If I have their entire genomes, I can look at locations on the gene to see what in the world these people might be like. What, in the name of God, is in this genetic mix? Even if I can examine two of these profiles, it would be enough to go public. I mean, I'm sorry to be so excited about this, but as far as evolutionary biology goes, I can't imagine a bigger discovery. To say nothing of the global religious and political implications of a race of intelligent nonhumans among us. What I'm saying is, if we can map the genome of even two of them, I can make some determinations about what it means that they are *not* human. What are they?"

Sam looked at his phone again. Two missed calls from Nguyen.

"I can get you a fresh sample from Alexi and Riker the fastest, and probably Tawana. A few days to collect them, and I can overnight them back to Juliana. Can this be kept private?"

"The answer, unfortunately, is sort of," William said. "In order to type the genome, I need a release from the individuals to comply with the university's ethics policy concerning the use of human subjects for research, and I would need to open a formal study. And I can't promise that no one else in the department would find out."

"Can't we fly it under the radar?'

"Possibly, but if I sequence a genome on the sly without opening a formal study, the results won't be usable or publishable. There would be no controls or accreditation."

"But you could see the results?"

"Basically, yes. I'll get you my lab assistant's contact information. He can start the sequencing right away. I'll tell him it's private—for now." William paused. "But I could use something else from you."

"Okay."

"Juliana says you have an old journal. Something you think applies to this inquiry."

"I'll email it to you. But it's not for public consumption. And I've got a question."

"Fire away."

"How can these genes survive from one generation to the next? Positing the hypothetical that sometime, way back when, creatures were bred by humans and another race—say, aliens, Sasquatch, whatever you want to say."

"Not my field," William said, "but I've studied genomic properties related to inherited brain traits, so I can help out a little here. Genetic genealogy is odd. It doesn't work the way people think it does. Put it this way; you know how once in a while you'll hear about someone who's a descendant, let's say, of George Washington? How it's talked about as though maybe the person shares traits with the famous ancestor?"

"Like the Daughters of the American Revolution."

"Right. That's all bullshit," William said. "If you go back four or five generations, the genes are so diluted that you really don't share any meaningful genetic codes with your predecessors. At the great, great, great grandparent level, you've got sixty-four parental ancestors, and that doubles with every generation. By the time you get back to, I guess, the aliens to whom you refer, which I think you would place in ancient times, the number of progenitors would be in the trillions."

"How can that be? Since there's never been a trillion people?"

"The trillions thing presumes no inbreeding. But most human breeding, even up until today, *is* inbreeding at a closer level than you would imagine. We're all related. At least within broad geographic categories."

"But there's another explanation," Juliana said. "It's that the demon gene, the angel gene, the alien gene, whatever you call it, entered the scene much more recently."

"*Much* more recently," William said. "As in, Paradisi, Hightower, and company had a full breed as a *parent*."

Sam looked at his phone.

Land yet? Where are you? Amelia.

"Have you ever used one of those genetic companies to trace your origins, like 23 and Me, Ancestry.com?"

"God, no. They use that shit to catch criminals. What are you suggesting?"

"That we upload a couple of your samples to this company called Genematch. They find relatives for people who get typed by 23 and Me or whatever. You're trying to round these people up, right?"

Sam looked at his phone. *10:35 p.m.*

"I've got an appointment at eleven," he said. He motioned for the check.

"We'll be around," Juliana said.

"One last thing, for now," Sam said. "What about the final result? The other envelope?" The one from the Mt. Hermon dude.

"Oh, yeah," William said. "Nothing showed up. It's a little

weird, because there's some indication of genetic material, but no markers. No X, no Y. No alleles. A corrupted sample."

Sam stood, hugged Juliana, and extended his hand to William.

"Wait, Sam." Juliana held up a long, thin Q-tip.

Sam frowned.

"Your mother's one of them, right?"

Sam looked at his phone. "I'm running late. Tell you what, I don't like it, but I'll do the swab if you two meet me at my office in Virginia on Monday."

William and Juliana exchanged glances.

"You're not going to tell us why, are you?" Juliana said.

Sam did not respond.

"Never mind," she said. "Sometimes you don't know why."

Sam swabbed the inside of his cheeks, handed the swab back to Juliana, and turned toward the door. "I'm not trying to round them up, William. They're trying to round me up."

CHAPTER SEVEN

SAM STOOD IN FRONT of the Trinity Episcopal Cathedral in the heavy evening heat, perhaps exactly where his mother had stood fifty years earlier, trying to connect with the seventeen-year-old who hoped a wooden statute could answer her prayer.

His phone buzzed. 10:50. Amelia. *Decline.* The cathedral was open only until 11:00. Sam pocketed his phone, looked the colossal Gothic structure up and down one more time, and marched forward.

He walked up the three wide, deep steps and into the cathedral. No one sat in the pews. The vast hall was empty, at least the public area. He strode down the center aisle towards the altar. He wondered if the Jesus his mother confronted to no avail was the same Jesus he stared up at now. *As always with the Great One and his Son, nothing*, she had written so long ago. Up close, the carving was cruder than from a distance, the large features, hands, and feet roughly hewn in the old polished wood. It was, nevertheless, an ageless and beautiful piece of art. Jesus' eyes conveyed what the artist intended—a sad but hopeful gaze crafted to establish eye contact with observers from any reasonable angle. Jesus and his cross hung suspended from thin wires to the side of the altar. He was about twice the size of a regular person. His feet hung six feet from the floor, and his head, ringed by a crown of thick, unevenly spaced thorns, towered fifteen feet above.

"Maybe you did mean well," Sam said to the carving. "But if they're damned for being half human, where did you come from? And what about your own resurrection? It's a little hard to believe Calvary was your first rodeo. Like with the Connecticut Yankee's eclipse, did you have them fooled? 'Cheaply deceived,' as Twain put it. But if you were at least trying to do something good with it, why did you leave, and where have you been? Doesn't everyone have their story? Or is it not exactly *everyone*? Are you even in charge of anything? Were you ever?"

Sam stepped forward and placed an envelope containing the summons on Jesus' feet, where it rested between his feet and the wooden nail pinning them to the cross.

"You're served, amigo." Sam stepped back and looked up at Jesus.

And, as was never the case with the Great One and his Son, something.

• • •

Sam stood on the steps outside the cathedral and hit a number on his phone.

"Where the hell have you been?" Amelia's voice was cracking.

"Miami—you knew that. What's up?"

Tragedy. Roommate found her in apartment this afternoon. Relapse . . . overdose. Probably heroin.

Before Amelia got to the point, Sam saw where she was going. Farah.

For the first time as an adult, Sam screamed. The same word, again and again. Sometime during the screaming, someone gently clicked shut the cathedral doors. A moment later the towering building went dark.

The street looked empty, too empty for this early on a Friday night near downtown Miami. *Slow time, observe.* Sam breathed deeply to calm his beating heart. He turned right on Bayshore Drive towards the Hilton. Across the street and a little behind, a man walked quickly at Sam's pace. The man did not appear to be paying any particular attention to him. Sam glanced back at him and reached out. The guy was in his own head, which was hard to pick up on from sixty feet away.

Sam slowed a little and looked again. The man was putting way too much effort into not paying attention to him. And Sam was almost sure he carried a weapon. The man focused on the sidewalk ahead, but his attention centered on the bulge at his back. His safety, the tool of his trade. Maybe a knife, but probably a gun.

Sam took another turn, slipping out of the man's sightline. The Hilton was only a long city block away. Sam sat on one of a group of benches near enough to the corner for the man to see him quickly. He steeled his mind, focused, and watched the man turn the corner—his eyes meeting Sam's. He kept moving, but not without an almost imperceptible stutter step.

"Why are you following me?" Sam asked softly when the man began to pass him on the sidewalk. He knew the man could simply walk up and kill him.

The man stopped, turned to Sam, glared menacingly for a moment, and then smirked. He stepped closer. "Am I that obvious?"

"Not really."

"Yeah, I heard you were good like that. I'm protecting you, bro." He extended his hand. "Jimmie Butarab."

Sam shook it. "Steve sent you down here?"

"I live here. He called, yeah. And Mr. Young, I'll feel a lot better when you're back inside your hotel."

CHAPTER EIGHT

SAM, BACK AT THE hotel bar, listened intently to Amelia on the phone while Jimmie Buterab, on the stool next to him, sipped a club soda and watched the door.

"Nguyen talked to Detective Sharp, and I spoke briefly to Sparf," Amelia said. "Farah lived in a two-bedroom apartment with Moira, her roommate—a nursing student and a good friend. Moira saw her go to her room this afternoon and she never came out. It's not what you're thinking, Sam. She OD'd. Either accidentally or on purpose, but whatever happened, *she* did it—not someone else, and not because of you."

"Farah's not an opioid addict," Sam said. "She got caught with Ecstasy. She's about to start college. She just got off probation. It makes no sense."

"You're not making sense, Sam. You're scaring me. We all cared about her. But after a year and a half of drug testing, she's finally off the hook. That's exactly when she might be tempted to use. And exactly when someone might overdo it. You've got to understand that this is what happened. Farah's death had nothing to do with you, and if you say it did, it's going to piss me off."

"I hear you," Sam said.

"When are you back?"

"About three tomorrow."

"See you then," Amelia said. "And Sam?"

"Yes?"

"I appreciate that, for whatever reason you're not fully explaining, you have bodyguards watching us at work and at home. But a bodyguard wouldn't've saved Farah. You see that, right?"

"I'll think about it."

Sam hung up. "Got a question for you, Jimmie."

Jimmie Buterab was sitting next to him at the Hilton bar sipping a club soda. "Shoot." Jimmie looked content, like a young guy without a worry in the world. He had an average, unassuming build, and no more than the normal amount of swagger for a tough guy in his mid-twenties, but his relaxed manner—particularly for someone who had likely been placed on high alert by Steve—bespoke an unseen strength. Jimmie faced the door. The bar was empty. He was happy to talk, or not.

"You've been told to keep an eye on me until I'm in my room, right?"

"Basically, yes."

"But what about after that?"

"I don't know. I'd probably text Steve. See what he wanted. My guess is if you keep your door locked, don't open it to strangers, all good. These hotels are fully covered by cameras, and everybody knows it. Pretty safe."

"If I decided to hang myself in my room, though? Or shoot up drugs, overdose. Or smash the window and jump out, you couldn't protect me from that, could you?"

"I guess not. But you're not going to harm yourself. You seem like more of a drinker, to be honest. Why are you asking me all this?"

"Sometimes I don't know why."

Jimmie stepped away from the bar with his phone, presumably to check in with Uncle Steve. Sam picked up his phone and saw a text from Juliana—William's assistant's contact information. *For Swabs.* Sam saved it and opened a web browser.

Genes. Genome. Violence. Empathy.
Crime gene.

A genetic analysis of 900 offenders from Finland has revealed two genes associated with violent crime. Those with these genetic markers were 13 times more likely to have a history of repeated violent behavior.

Sam texted Nguyen. *Buccal swabs from Riker, Esau, and Tawana. FedEx ASAP to below address.*

Jimmie placed a hand on Sam's back. "Hey, Bubba. Steve says I can bail if you're cool. You want a ride to the airport in the morning?

"Sure."

"See you down here at eight-thirty. And a word of advice, Sam."

"Yeah?"

"Don't go out, and don't drink too much."

Sam ordered one last cold shot of vodka, a double, and opened another web browser.

Mount Hermon. Resort. Summit.

Mount Hermon is a mountain cluster constituting the southern end of the Anti-Lebanon mountain range. Its summit straddles the border between Syria and Lebanon and, at 2,814 m above sea level, is the highest point in Syria. On the top, in the United Nations buffer zone between Syrian- and Israeli-occupied territories, is the highest permanently manned UN position in the world, known as "Hermon Hotel," located at 2,814 m altitude. The southern slopes of Mount Hermon extend to the Israeli-occupied portion of the Golan Heights, where the Mount Hermon Ski Resort is located, with a top elevation of 2,040 m. A peak in this area rising to 2,236 m is the highest elevation in Israeli-controlled territory.

Sam emailed the information to Nguyen. *I'll call you from the airport re: private tour of Hermon Hotel.* Sam's phone buzzed.

"Juliana?" Sam said. *Nothing.* "Juliana? Did you butt dial me?"

He heard her crying.

"Sam. I'm at the emergency room—can you come? I'm freaking out."

"What?"

"William collapsed at my apartment half an hour ago. I'm losing it. They're saying he had a mini-stroke or something."

• • •

Juliana sat next to Sam in the Uber SUV, headed towards her apartment. Sam removed his arm from around her and sent a text.

"He's only sixty-three years old," Juliana said. "I was just getting to know him, but he has no history of health conditions that I know about."

"I heard some of what the doctor said to you," Sam said "He's doing okay."

"How do people just suddenly have a stroke?!"

"A mini-stroke," Sam said.

The SUV turned into Juliana's apartment complex at 2:20 a.m. She looked at Sam, who had not said much more than those few words since he had arrived at the emergency room where Juliana had just finished speaking to the ER doctor.

"He's got kids," she said. "Plus the whole department. His friends. A brother. I don't know who to call. I don't know what to do."

"I don't either, Juliana. And I know you're not going to understand what I'm about to tell you, but I'm going to have someone protect you. Someone here."

Juliana stared straight ahead. For a long moment, neither she, nor Sam, nor the Uber driver spoke.

"Okay," she said, either understanding on some level the danger to which Sam was referring or, more likely, attributing his statement to a concern for her mental health.

A Lincoln Town Car eased next to the Uber, and Sam rolled down the window.

"I told you not to go out," Jimmie said.

CHAPTER NINE

DAY 3, FRIDAY, OCTOBER 4, 2019

Straight from the airport, Sam parked the Escalade, took the stairs two at a time up to his office, and whisked in just as his phone buzzed. It was 4:25 p.m. A blocked number. He glanced back and saw Nguyen, who leaned with his hand on the doorjamb, his normally alert visage replaced by a sunken face and bloodshot eyes.

"This is Young."

"Good evening, Samson. Nice job in Florida."

Sam hit the recording application on his phone. The male voice from the other end was the same one he initially identified as Eastern European two days before. But what was the origin of the accent?

"It seems you may have made some progress with our plan," the voice said.

"Our plan? You still won't tell me who you are."

"I'm someone who cares about you and appreciates what you're doing."

"We've never met," Sam said. "All I'm doing is a case I was hired to do, and not by you."

"I appreciate it all the same. And to the extent that this matters, we have, indeed, met."

The leathery voice polished its words. A little like the concierge at the kind of hotel where the staff considers itself superior to the guests. On a transcript the words would appear deferential, polite. In spoken form, they sought to dominate and command. It was more like the voice of an attorney truly gifted in courtroom oratory. Arguing with the voice would be like fighting the wind.

Sam glanced up at Nguyen, still slouched in the doorway.

"Mr. Young, are you still there?"

"When? When did we meet?"

"You'll find out all you need to know soon."

"When?"

"At the opportune—"

Sam hung up. He pulled up the recording from his app. *Click, click, send.*

"Does whoever that was have any idea what you're planning?" Nguyen said. "'Cause I can't say I do."

"That guy understands pretty much everything . . . Rough night?"

"Not really."

"What'd you do?"

"Not much. Drank beer and watched a documentary about abused children with this chick I'm dating. She cried."

"She was sad about the movie?"

"No. But I'm ready to butter Vick's biscuit. I've got something new."

"Let's have it."

"His girlfriend used to sell jade eggs for a living. Like by holding events at people's homes, that kind of thing. About two months ago, her jade egg business was purchased for three hundred and fifty thousand dollars by a Miami company whose main business appears to be travel-related—for example, they own two resorts and a cruise ship."

"First, what's a jade egg, and second, so what?"

"So what is that Vick's assets were mostly frozen by the government when he got arrested. Under his cooperation agreement, he can't engage in a financial transaction involving more than ten thousand dollars without the government's permission. His girlfriend just sold a small company that can't be worth twenty grand for more than ten times that to a company that has no reason to be interested in jade eggs."

"All right, what's a jade egg?"

"A polished ceramic egg-shaped object that women put in their vaginas to increase blood flow and strengthen the muscles. They walk around with the egg inside, and it's supposed to awaken sexual sensitivity and stuff. The eggs are supposed to make chicks feel calm or horny or something. Both, I think. My point is that no jade egg business is worth three-fifty K. You can get 'em online for forty bucks, and tons of independent contractors compete for the business."

"Sounds like you know a lot about jade eggs."

"I bought one at a sex party with this chick I dated."

"Did it work?"

"It fell out whenever I took a shit."

"I walked right into that."

"The Miami company that bought the business is partly owned by a guy named Anthony Yukov, a Ukrainian and—ready for the kicker?"

Sam folded his arms.

"Anthony Yukov is Igor Alexi's cousin. Weird, huh?"

Sam did not respond.

"So what's a relative of our client, against whom Vick is fabricating evidence in a death-penalty case, doing by essentially gifting huge money to Vick by buying a jade egg company from his girlfriend?"

"Hmm. I'm really distracted right now. Put it together for me."

"What I think is that Igor's trying to buy Vick off, to get him not to testify, or to deliberately screw up or something. The question is, do we do anything about it? And the answer, I think, is no."

"You're getting good."

"Thanks, Sam."

The two stood in silence for a long moment, watching the floor.

"But actually, I think you wanted me here today for something different."

Sam sat and leaned back in his chair. He took a series of deep breaths. *Slow time. Observe.*

"I'm feeling a little lost. I don't know, I guess I feel like—"

"Like what, boss?"

Sam stared out the window, across the plaza towards the courthouse. "Can you drive down to Delilah's, find this Appalachian dude Esau Jacobs, and bring him up here?"

"I can try. What else?"

"Can you try to find Barnabus?"

"Why?"

"Not sure yet."

Sam punched some keys on his computer and looked up at Nguyen.

"Anything else?" Nguyen said.

"Yeah, and I need you to use some of your best sleuthing on this."

"Sounds filthy."

"The last person executed in Virginia was Demetrius Kilpatrick, in 2018; before that it was Jenkin Ryan, 2017."

"Okay."

"The Department of Corrections is really secretive about its execution protocols. A small group from the public can watch the execution, but they immediately drop a curtain after a doctor declares the prisoner dead. The results of the autopsies are kept under seal."

"Autopsies? Isn't the cause of death kind of obvious at that point?"

"They do them anyway. What I want to know is, how long after the death do the autopsies happen these days, where do they happen, who does them, and under what level of security?"

Nguyen nodded. "Do you know where I should begin? I mean, to avoid seeming like a serious creeper?"

"I was thinking you could start with this." Sam hit send on his phone to text a press article.

"I'm sorry, but I gotta ask. I assume this is about Igor. But why? If you're so worried about his execution, why not work out a deal? Avoid the death penalty?"

Sam did not reply.

"If you're not gonna let us in on what you're up to, I hope you get the help you need from someone," Nguyen said. "Like maybe this person you just talked to. The ski trip guy. The one who knows everything. Even if you don't know exactly who he is."

"He's not a person," Sam said.

Nguyen started to leave the room, but stopped and turned back. "Whatever he is, maybe he licked that envelope."

"You are getting good," Sam said, but Nguyen was already gone.

CHAPTER TEN

SAM WALKED TOWARDS THE Escalade and hit the key remote. He climbed in and tossed his briefcase on the passenger seat, and then pulled the thin *Book of I Enoch* volume out of his briefcase and flipped through some of his highlighted passages.

To Michael the Lord said, Go and announce to Azazel his crimes, and to other Angels who are with them who have been associated with women, that they are polluted . . . and bind them for seventy generations underneath the Earth. (Book of I Enoch, Chapter XI:15–18)

Sam opened a document on his phone.

70 generations.
Psalms 90:10: A generation is seventy years.
70 x 70. 4900 years?

Enoch born 3424 BCE Walks with God/taken to Heaven at age 365.

3,059 BCE plus 4900. 1841 CE?

And I Enoch XV:8:

Now the demons, who have been born of the union of spirit and flesh, shall be called evil spirits upon the Earth, and Earth shall be their habitation.

His phone buzzed. "Tawana?"

"The prosecutor wasn't too happy the other day."

"I hear you." Sam was suddenly so tired—for him, an unaccustomed feeling. His eyes roamed the parking lot. He thought back to four years ago, when he fell asleep in his car the day Camille was arrested.

"We've got business," Tawana said, "me and you. Skiing is gonna be hazardous to your health."

"I may be booking a trip for you, too. Come by the office tomorrow. Let's talk about it."

"You'll see me when you see me. Or you won't. Bye, Samson."

"Bye, Salome."

Salome Tawana Hightower Ortiz breathed into the phone before hanging up without a response.

CHAPTER ELEVEN

AMELIA AND SAM SAT at Harpoon Hannah's. A cold shot of vodka sat on the bar in front of Sam. Amelia sipped a beer, facing him from her barstool with her normal expression. Serious and sincere.

"I wanted to talk because I'm still pissed at you for telling me not to do death-penalty cases in the first place," Amelia said. "And now that we have the right deal, you're acting weird about it."

"I know. Sorry. You followed your instincts and ignored me."

"Yeah, but I almost listened to you. And if I had—"

"I get it. You should ignore me more often."

"Believe me, I do."

"Ha. Look, you're the best lawyer around here, and you don't get enough credit for it. This firm has not only won six acquittals in big cases in four years, we've also had a ridiculous number of pretrial dismissals based on your work. People around here do know it. I'm sorry about how I've been acting lately. Things have been . . . weird."

Amelia pulled out a file—*Igor Alexi*. It consisted of her personal file on the case, which represented a fraction of the data Sparf had provided them in discovery, the documents from their own investigation, and the legal filings.

"You represented Muldoon, and he didn't get the death penalty," Sam said. "And thanks to that, you, and therefore we, were personally requested as counsel by Igor Alexi. An even scarier case."

Sam knew Amelia fully comprehended his comment about Igor having a scary case. Igor Alexi faced the death penalty for the brutal murder and alleged robbery of his estranged wife. But the government had no conclusive forensic evidence and no eyewitnesses. The trial rested on circumstantial evidence— each piece of which could be argued either way—and the sketchy confession to Clifford Vick. The case was scary not because of the crime, but because, based on the evidence, Igor could actually be innocent.

"What I'm asking is why you suddenly think Igor should risk his life," Amelia said. "Months ago, I thought we wanted the plea—at least to try to get him to take it."

Sam looked at Amelia. "I'm sorry. Just give me a few days to think about it."

"The trial's Monday, Sam. I'm working on it every day, and you should be, too."

"I'll figure it out soon."

Sam's phone buzzed. An email from eLocal. Two leads.

Fairfax, Virginia. "I have been charged with reckless driving and need to retain a traffic lawyer. The police officer lied about how fast I was going, and I have a clean record. I can be reached at . . .

Decline lead. Click.

Cancel the fucking ski trip.

"I want to go see Igor," Amelia said.

Sam finished his drink. "You're his lawyer. You have every right to."

"But we're usually on the same page, at least about what we think a client should do. And now we're not."

"Go see Igor. See what you think he wants."

"I will."

"Amelia," Sam said, as she turned to walk out. "Be careful."

She narrowed her eyes, like when he suggested a screwy trial tactic that, to a diligent, conscientious attorney, made no sense.

"Why?"

CHAPTER TWELVE

SAM SLID THE ESCALADE into park and gazed across the trimmed lawn of the cemetery. He walked up the slight incline across the grass. He always visited at dusk for no particular reason. As he approached the grave, he always thought about how he walked just above the dead, the skeletons, resting in their coffins. The individual graves were adorned with no artificial lighting, but the light from the small black lampposts flanking the narrow road though the Garden of Serenity was sufficient to illuminate the inscriptions on each marker along the way towards his mother's. Having visited the grave for nineteen years, he felt like he knew the people. Jonathan Mitchell, 1925–1989. Philip Peterson, 1930–1991. Gladys Peterson, 1935–2015. *Were you alone so long, Gladys, or did you remarry?* And finally his mother, Marcela Young, 1955–2000. His mother's grave was no different from the others except that her gravestone inscriptions—

the name, the dates—and the implicit claim that the stone marked a grave were all lies. And yet Sam kept coming.

Where are you, Fifika?

Sam smelled an odor that conjured up a memory of a park ranger at Yellowstone National Park lecturing his group about grizzly bears. "You'll probably smell one before you see it. It's a smell like nothing else." Or maybe it wasn't a smell at all, but something else, like the auras his mother described in her journal.

I knew by now that sometimes what I experience as a sense of smell is not about scents at all, but little glimpses into the past. The smell of fresh flowers follows a happy woman, a waft of feces surrounds drunks and liars, and a lemony icy scent marks places of safety and generosity. The monkey-cage smell meant suffering has occurred here. It also surrounds those filled with hate. Like Miguel.

Sam's head smashed against the top of his mother's gravestone, and then nothing. When he came to, Tawana Hightower sat next to him, holding a wet towel to his temple.

"You hit me?" Sam said.

"No, Bubba. But I may have saved you. Though why, I'm not so sure."

Tawana pulled the towel away and Sam felt the side of his head, expecting a huge welt, but felt nothing but wetness from the towel. He looked at his hand— blood. Tawana stood and placed her palm on the gravestone. She traced the words that spelled his mother's name with her index finger.

"That wasn't her name back then," she said. "But I guess you know that."

Sam did not reply, but looked all around him across the empty graveyard.

"What just happened?"

"You sure you want to know?"

"Yes."

"He smashed your head against the grave so hard I thought it killed you. Then I chased him off. When I came back, you were sitting here."

"You were following me?"

"Honey, lots of folks are following you."

"I don't think so. I would know."

"You'd know if *people* were following you, but—"

"I get it. So, who tried to kill me?"

"I don't know what he calls himself now."

"He's afraid of *you*?"

Tawana smiled. "Not of me. Afraid of bein' seen. He's a loner and he's gotten pretty crazy lately. He can scramble like a speedy little monkey, which is what he did when I yelled out to him. But what I'm trying to figure out was whether he was trying to kill you or scare you. And to me, that question turns on whether you can be killed, but we don't know the answer to that, do we? You think you just died and came back?"

"How does that feel?"

"Hard to describe."

"Try."

Tawana just looked away.

"So, who is he?" Sam said.

"Just another lost soul," she said. "Same as me."

"That's not what I asked."

"Sure it is."

Sam stood, brushed off his clothes, and ran his hand lightly over the top of his mother's gravestone.

"I didn't die. You healed me, that's all. I've been reading that journal for four years. You people can do shit like that."

"I loved her, Sam, and I like you. Because of that, I'm giving you some time to come to your senses about this ski trip. I like things how they are, Bubba."

It was completely dark now, and Tawana's face was barely visible as she stood in front of him, hand on her hip. But her eyes, almost possessed of their own light, bore into him, and he could feel her dancing in his head and put up no resistance. Tawana, so haggard and used up by life on the witness stand only days ago, gleamed like a star in the moonless sky, shining down on her first love's phony grave. She was beautiful, like Camille. Though they bore no other resemblance.

They walked together towards the Escalade, and Sam saw that Tawana had parked a beat-up Honda Civic behind it.

"Do you at least know what this guy looks like, Salome?"

Tawana opened her car door, appearing to deliberately ignore the question, got in and began to drive away. Her window rolled down as she passed him. "That's Tawana to you, Bubba. And I sure do. But you don't."

Sam watched the little car cruise around the corner, out of the Garden of Serenity, and down the main drag of the cemetery.

• • •

Sam sat in the parking lot of Church of the Holy Angels. He recalled when he was here the day after Camille was killed. He chugged a bottle of water, tossed it behind him, lifted his briefcase from the passenger floorboard, and stepped out of the Escalade. It was around eleven, and despite the late hour, sweat rose to his skin as he chirped the Escalade locked and approached the house at the far end of the parking lot.

Sam knocked but heard no response. Of course, Paul could be asleep, and Anna Buterab was almost surely gone for the evening, but Paul had always been a night owl. Sam knocked again and gazed back across the Holy Angels parking lot. Only Paul's pickup truck. No Anna. Nothing.

Sam's heart began to pound as he looked from window to window. The living-room light shone brightly through the shades and over the bushes lining the front of the priest's house. Sam stood silently on the stoop for a moment and then turned the knob and walked in, instinctively turning left, towards the light. He crossed to the center of the room and saw Andrada lying flat on the long couch, the same couch where Sam had strategized with Camille the night before her arrest four years before. He knew he had to call 911 and then Anna Buterab, but before doing so or checking Andrada's pulse, he simply stood in the center of the room looking at the man. He knew for certain that Andrada was dead.

Sam's phone buzzed.

"Sam?"

Sam turned. Alifair stood at the bottom of the stairs.

"I can't sleep," she said.

CHAPTER THIRTEEN

DAY 4, SATURDAY, OCTOBER 5, 2019

Sam had spent hours on a bench with Alifair dozing on his lap, her arms around him. He'd then waited several more hours before being interviewed by detectives about finding Andrada's body. The next morning, he parked the Escalade in the strip mall parking lot at the north edge of Bennet County and began to scroll through an article on his phone. It buzzed.

"This is Young."

"Hello, Mr. Young," Chief O'Malley said. "Been a while. I thought I'd call to suggest that you don't stray too far from your normal haunts these next few days. I know the priest was your friend, but if his death is found to be suspicious for any reason, we may need to talk."

Sam could tell O'Malley had wanted to say, *I just may detain your ass.*

"Anything else?" Sam said.

"Who's taking custody of that kid?"

Sam hung up and stepped out of the Escalade directly in front of Capital MMA just as the door to the martial arts fitness studio opened.

"You're stalking me now?" Amelia said.

"Stalking, no."

"So, you just show up outside my jujitsu class on a Saturday morning? You think this is the only time of the week I'll be too tired to kick your ass?" Amelia smiled, but the edge in her voice was real.

"I was in the neighborhood. Killing some time before a meeting."

"You okay?"

"Paul Andrada died last night."

"Oh, Sam. I'm sorry. Oh my God, what about—"

"I know. She's with Anna. I'm figuring it out."

"Contact Judge Chan. We can move the trial. Sparf won't object, and—"

"Not possible," Sam said. "How was your meeting with Igor?"

"I already know Igor's case has something to do with all the craziness from four years ago. You think I'm clueless? Like I can't look at the DNA result by now and figure it out?"

"So, how'd it go?'

"Well, you know I can't read minds or see magic shit like you. I'm basically a normal, healthy person and all."

"Very true."

"So instead of dodging and weaving around everything, I just asked him."

"Creative. And?"

"And I think you, Igor, and that nut Paradisi are probably all crazy. But Nguyen and I decided a long time ago that for whatever reason, we were going to see you through this. The annoying part is that you still act so mysterious about it. You can just tell us what's going on and why you do certain things. Both of us are a little worried about you. Relax. And besides—"

Sam put his phone in his pocket and hugged her. "Besides what?"

"We don't have to believe in any of this stuff anyway. It's all narratives, right? You taught me that. So, what's next?"

"Something would help for tomorrow. You know all that method-of-execution research you did early in the case? About the botched lethal injection and everything?"

"Yeah."

"You told me about the inmate who survived a lethal injection," Sam said. "Because the drugs were wrong or messed up. About how he suffered excruciating pain but lived?"

"Tyler Montgomery, Oklahoma."

"You said something about how his lawyers argued that since the state tried to kill him once and failed, it should not be permitted to try again. Remember?"

"Of course."

"What happened with that?"

"The courts ruled the state gets as many tries as it takes."

"Okay. I want you to write a motion about this issue. Arguing that the State should get only one shot at an execution. And make it something that will attract attention. Stretch it. Go as far out on a limb as you want. Back in the old days, if the hang rope broke, didn't the prisoner go free?"

"It's not a winning argument."

"I know. Thanks." Sam opened the door of the Escalade.

"Sam," Amelia said softly. "Asking me to write a motion about methods of execution for a guy pleading not guilty and going to trial in a few days makes no sense. Even if we lose, there'll be years of appeals before the execution would happen. Plus, we have so much other work to do. What you're asking makes no sense . . . and you know it."

Amelia narrowed her eyes and Sam looked away. Earnest complaints about his strange legal strategies had characterized their dynamic for years, but this was not one of them.

"What you and Igor want to do is pretty fucked up," she said. "But I'll draft what you're asking for. It'll be a motion to declare the death penalty unconstitutional, as violative of the Eighth Amendment—cruel and unusual punishment—unless the court orders that in the event Igor is sentenced to death, the State has only one shot at executing him, be it with lethal injection or the electric chair, the only methods allowed in Virginia. I'll cite all the methods-of-execution stuff about the times the injection drugs or an electric chair has failed and the recent lower court ruling from Oklahoma against us, and I'll toss in some historical British and Wild West BS about how people who survived an execution attempt were freed. The press will love it, which is what I think you're going for."

"Thanks." Sam's eyes softened.

"And I'll answer your next question too. It takes at least five years, sometimes much longer, for someone to be executed after a verdict of death in Virginia. There's direct appeal. Cert petition to the US Supreme Court on appeal. Then state *habeas corpus*. Then federal *habeas corpus*. Appeals on those. Barring something unusual, and if all of that fails, the sentencing court then sets an execution date within sixty days. The last-ditch effort of a clemency petition to the governor, which often gets decided right before the execution date."

"What if the defendant waives his appeals and *habeas corpus*?" Sam asked.

"I've never heard of that happening. But from what I do know, even if the defendant tries to waive all remedies, there's an automatic appeal on the issue of whether the death sentence was imposed arbitrarily and on a few other issues."

"So how long? The fastest?"

"I'd say nine months."

"You okay going along with this?" Sam said.

Amelia tossed her gym bag into the back seat of her car and then turned back to Sam. "Everybody has their story." she said. "And these aren't even people, right?"

• • •

Sam parked in front of his office.

Tap, tap, tap. "Mr. Young, you're a hard man to catch up with."

"Hey, Bernie." Sam's phone read 8:40 a.m. "How about Turnstiles Coffee Shop?"

Sam knew from vast previous experience that the coffee shop around the corner from the jail served beer, even in the morning. He took a long pull from one while he watched Bernie Genoa meticulously flavor his coffee—two Equals and a squirt of syrup—before sitting across from Sam, taking a sip, and opening a file.

"I've been hired to provide you some information," Bernie said.

"Make it quick, please. I got a murder trial Monday, which I hope you understand is why I've been so busy. But okay, hired by who?"

"Actually Sam, I suspect that is not why you have been so busy. Who I work for is not something you need to know, except to say that he, or she, is willing to spend quite a lot to make sure you have this information. For simplicity's sake, I'll use the pronoun *they* to refer to my client, but you should not take that to mean anything."

"Bernie, come on," Sam said. "No disrespect, but you're a court-appointed guardian *ad litem*. If one of your wards has something to do with one of my cases, out with it."

Bernie frowned and focused on the first page in his file. "I think you should hear me out. I've been told that if you had listened to me days ago, a good deal of trouble could have been avoided. Your selfish decisions are affecting others."

Sam sipped his beer but did not reply. Sam pushed his mind at Bernie, but just a touch. He still got the answer, plain as day. Bernie had no idea what the information he had really meant.

"You may want to write some of this down. I have names and some dates, but I have been clearly instructed not to provide you with any documents. A lot of what I'm telling you, though, is documented to my reasonable satisfaction, and I've been doing social histories for a while now. For guardian cases, and—"

"That's okay, Bernie. I'm listening. I'll remember."

"Okay, my client wants you to know that all of this information is accurate, even the undocumented portions. Much of the information is not accompanied by dates, just so you know. But that does not mean, according to my client, that they are not in possession of more specific information."

"I'm ready," Sam said, glancing at the time on his phone.

"First, we have Jonathon Williamson." Bernie placed a picture of Esau Jacobs in front of Sam. It was a photo taken from the side of Esau Jacobs at the counter of a store of some sort. "My client wants you to know that Mr. Williamson committed four brutal killings of young women in Southwest Virginia and North Carolina many years ago. The murders were similar because, in each of them, the woman was either decapitated or had her face removed. Authorities never linked them. I have a 1982 newspaper article about one of the unsolved murders. Would you like to see it?"

"No, thanks."

"Does Williamson mean anything to you?"

"No."

"Next, we have Riker Lugnudsky, born in 1989 in Lexington, Kentucky. I'm pretty sure this guy is still alive and that your firm represents him. My client would like you to know that he is a sadist and serial rapist who has forced himself on women regularly since college. Only one case was ever reported, and I have some records on that, but no charges filed. More recently, he forcibly sodomized a woman in her apartment after an internet date, but she never reported it."

"How do you know any of this? I mean, the unreported items?"

"I've been hired to convey information. Riker Lugnudsky is not a good person. I'm sure the fact that one of your clients is a sociopath is hardly breaking news to you, but there you have it."

Bernie's voice had picked up a little edge, as though he was beginning to enjoy delivering the volatile news. *And why not?* Sam guessed this little conversation was the most lucrative half hour of Bernie's career. Sam sipped his beer, focusing on Bernie. *Slow time. Observe.*

"Next, we've got Salome Ortiz. A Tunisian born in Germany in 1945. She's pushing eighty by now. She spent years as a prostitute in Budapest and worked as a hired assassin for drug dealers. She's murdered three people, one by poison and two by slitting their throats after, or during, sex. Not sure where she is now. Ring a bell?"

"Is that it?"

"Nope. The prize of the litter is Trinity Kritalsh. A gypsy from Argentina who ran away from home in the fifties and committed upwards of twenty murders as she travelled around South America, living a grifter's life. She was also a prostitute who often wound up being her clients' last lay. No information on where she is now. But my client would like you to know that Trinity Kritalsh is not a good person."

Bernie looked up with a grim smile. "Is any of this interesting to you?"

"Maybe."

"Finally, my client wants you to know that Kritalsh's sister, Fifika Kritalsh, though not as bad as her sister, murdered four people in the fifties, including her own stepfather and a policeman in Argentina. She also sold drugs and prostituted herself regularly until she had a son in 1982. I understand that she eventually disappeared and hasn't been seen by her son, or anyone, for almost twenty years. Strike a chord?"

"Anything else?"

"I have now almost fulfilled my obligation to my client."

"There's more?" Sam said.

"Just one thing. My client said to tell you they acknowledge receipt."

"And?"

"I didn't ask," Bernie said. "What do you think they mean by it? Acknowledge receipt? Of what? That you shouldn't be serving my client with anything without my knowledge? I thought you didn't even know who they were."

Sam finished his beer and stood.

"What do *you* think this case is about, Bernie?'

"I think some important people want you to stop associating with scumbags."

CHAPTER FOURTEEN

DAY 5, SUNDAY, OCTOBER 6, 2019

Sam had met Farah's mother only once. The brief conversation had happened at the Bennet County Courthouse on the day he and Amelia had handled her daughter's sentencing hearing. At twenty, Farah had been living at home at the time of her arrest, an event that had, according to Farah, jarred her traditional Lebanese family. Farah swore that her father, who had died just the year before, would have disowned her had he still been alive. Sam had doubted that, though he surmised that the volatility of her father's reaction would have been driven less by her drug use and more by the fact that she had been arrested with a young white man in a parked car late at night.

Maybe Farah bristled a bit under the norms of Lebanese culture, which suggested a woman her age should focus on marriage and children, or at least on her education. Or maybe she had simply not outgrown the partying lifestyle that accompanies waiting tables at a popular bar, an endeavor her parents had surely detested. In any event, Sam had never spoken more than a few sentences to Laila, even that day at the courthouse. Farah's case had been a simple one with an easy, predictable result. Eighteen months probation, then dismissal. That Farah had overdosed the day after probation ended and immediately before embarking on her journey to a prestigious college would go down in courthouse lore as a typical example of the scourge of addiction.

But as Sam met Laila's eyes across the mosque, he knew instantly that she, like him, did not buy a bit of it. He winced inside, aware that he should have reached out to Laila right after hearing the news instead of merely showing up like a regular guest at the funeral, as if he did not appreciate the inestimable magnitude of Laila's loss. As if he had been no one special in Farah's life. Laila would never be able to understand Sam's true thoughts about Farah's death, and it would be beyond foolishness to attempt to explain it to her. But the thoughts remained.

One of Laila's friends spoke from the lectern at the front of the mosque. Sam looked over at Amelia, who cried openly, and then to Nguyen on his other side, who simply stared at the floor.

When they filed out, Sam stood aside and let the guests trudge past. The mosque took a long time to empty out. Laila, the last to walk back up the aisle, her arm around an older gentleman, stopped in front of Sam.

They hugged, but Sam could tell it was a cursory gesture, a forced move for Laila.

"I'm so sorry, Laila," Sam said.

Laila gestured for her companion to go on ahead.

"You know what happened?" Laila asked.

"I know she overdosed on fentanyl. Heroin and fentanyl."

"She didn't do heroin or fentanyl," Laila said.

"I know," Sam said.

Laila, whose dry eyes must have grown sick of crying, tilted her head quizzically at Sam, as if to suggest he was missing the obvious.

"This had something to do with you, Sam. With your work. She never should have been working with criminals. It was not for her."

Before descending the steps towards the rest of the grieving family, Laila turned to Sam again and spoke with soft but forceful words, conveying advice, or a warning, or maybe nothing on purpose at all except a strong personal belief about the world.

"You were never her kind of people."

Nguyen and Amelia leaned against the Escalade as Sam approached. He watched them speak to each other as he closed the distance, reaching out with his mind to see if he could decipher the topic, or at least the tone, of their conversation. *Eavesdropping*, he supposed. The question between them was easy to read. *Do you think he's losing it?*

• • •

Sam parked the Escalade in front of the office. He pulled up a web browser and quickly found what he was looking for.

Father Paul Andrada, 72, died of a stroke inside his home at Holy Angels Catholic Church in Bennet County yesterday, October 4, 2019. He was born in Argentina. He and his sister emigrated from Argentina to Miami in 1959. He became a priest in Washington, DC, in 1975 and served in various parishes until coming to Holy Angels in 1984, where he served as pastor until his death. He is predeceased by his sister, Marcela Young, who died in a plane crash in 2000. A memorial service will be held at Holy Angels on October 12 at 10 a.m.

Beep, beep.

CHRISTOPHER LEIBIG   91

Sam looked up. A red van sat next to him, idling in the wrong lane, and for just a second, his heart jumped. *You bulletproof now, too?* But instead of a gun blast, he saw the smiling face of Riker Lugnudsky.

"Hey, Riker."

"Hi, Sam. And you can call me Lug Nut." He winked. "Nguyen said you wanted me to stop by soon. Not sure why. Wouldn't you know, I just did a delivery at your office."

"I'm sure I had a reason. How about tomorrow? Three p.m. here."

"Sure, Sam. I appreciate what you did with my case, but I gotta tell you, whatever you guys are up to now, I don't love it."

• • •

Sam took the stairs to his office. Nguyen sat at the reception station previously manned by Farah. Flowers of various types and combinations covered her desk.

"Hey, boss, there's a lot going on. And I admit that's a wacky comment to make when we have a death-penalty trial starting tomorrow, but I'm not even referring to that."

Sam followed Nguyen down the hall to the closed door of the investigator's office.

"He likes free internet," Nguyen said, hand on the doorknob of his office. "You should know, he's strapped with an old mini-pistol. I didn't ask why."

Sam opened the door to Esau slowly clicking keys on Nguyen's computer. "Hi, Mr. Jacobs."

"Hello, Samson."

Esau's long gray hair and thick beard accentuated his blue eyes, which peered sidelong and only fleetingly at Sam. A close look at Esau belied one's superficial assessment that he was a mindless drifter or merely an eccentric recluse. The flickering eyes hiding under the scruffy gray brows conveyed something else: *I'm not one of those who can easily hide. But I can hide.*

"I'm a little busy right now, got a murder case starting tomorrow. Do you mind if we catch up after court? I may be able to help you."

Esau watched Sam and then glanced back at the computer screen. "I was always a patient man. Not feeling that way so much anymore."

"He's staying at the Hilton around the corner," Nguyen said. "I got him a burner phone, too."

"Okay. Esau, I'll check in later."

Sam and Nguyen closed the door on Esau and turned the corner into Amelia's office.

"Your execution motion's ready," Amelia said. "And I'm ready to hit send to Lexi Shapiro. It's a go?"

"Yep," Sam said.

"Believe it or not," Nguyen said, "on the way down to get Esau yesterday afternoon, I was able to find Reginald Caffrey in Lynchburg, Virginia. You know who that is?"

"No."

"He's been in the press. He was on Virginia's execution team—they really call it that by the way—from 1992 to 2011. He helped conduct sixty-two executions in his time. He's a minister now and speaks out against the death penalty. I caught up with him after his Saturday evening prayer group. Anyway, he was willing to talk to me about autopsies. He had nothing to do with them, but he did stay with the bodies until they were secured and transported to the medical examiner's office, which always happens the same night as the execution. The prison has no storage facilities for bodies. The bodies are transported in body bags in the back of a state police wagon with an escort. At least three troopers are on the detail. It's done in secret, of course, to avoid being ceremoniously followed by haters, supporters, whatever. They go to the district office of the medical examiner in Roanoke. From there, the autopsies are done like all others—

forthwith. According to Caffrey, by the next morning. Based on a couple of press articles that announced autopsy results, that seems right. Nothing is done to the bodies before the autopsy. The protocol is that once the doctor at the prison declares death, everything else is chain-of-custody protocol. The next person to open that bag is the medical examiner."

"Does Caffrey happen to know how the body coolers work?"

"At the ME in Roanoke? No clue. Didn't ask. How would he?"

"Thanks, Nguyen. I guess I should see what's in my office."

"Or maybe get ready for tomorrow?" Amelia said.

"That, too."

Sam began to leave the room, and turned back to his friends.

"Sorry about all the craziness going on."

Amelia and Nguyen exchanged glances.

"He thinks we're morons," Amelia said. And then, to Sam, "You worried about the geezer packin' heat?"

"A little." The three of them stood in Amelia's office with eyes downcast. Sam saw the juror list for Igor Alexi's trial laid out on her desk next to her witness binders and stacks of police reports and transcripts. Long after it became awkward, Amelia ended the silence.

"You guys wanna talk demonology?"

• • •

Sam parked in front of the Bennet County Detention Center and checked a missed call on his phone. *Juliana, 9:25.* Jail visits stopped at 10:00. Igor, though expecting to see Sam the night before his trial, would be understanding. On the other hand, *not* visiting a client in jail the day before a big trial was not Sam's style.

Sam's phone buzzed again at the entryway to the jail.

"Hey, Juliana. How's it going down there?"

"We're okay. Thought you may want to know that William is at home and doing really well. Believe it or not, he still wants to come tomorrow. He received Nguyen's package yesterday and has been on the phone trying to get the testing going . . . I'm glad you were here the other night."

"Of course. That's great news about William."

"About tomorrow—won't you be in the middle of a trial?"

Sam approached the metal detector. He had almost no time left to see Igor before visitation ended. "Sort of."

• • •

"Sorry I'm late, Igor. We have, like, five minutes."

Igor plopped into his seat across from Sam in the visiting booth. "All good, Samson. Raj visited me today. I feel fine. I'm ready. Really. Don't stress out. You seem all wound up. You can't solve everything."

"It sounds like you've been listening to Raj."

"I'm all set for tomorrow. I trust you."

"Thanks, Igor. That means a lot. My worry is whether you're ready. No second thoughts?"

"I'll tell you, when I first died and came back, it felt amazing. It was like, you ever seen the movie *Highlander*? That Scottish guy who can't die, when he realizes it? They called it *the quickening*. He's standing on the beach and he lets the soul of a stag into his heart and runs like the wind. It was like that when I realized who I was, my heartbeat with the animal energy of all of creation. My soul ran like the wind. But when you get older, it changes. With each resurrection you can see more, do more, but at the same time the excitement of it, the rush, even the regular joy of living dwindles. And eventually you're so terribly alone. It's like a deal with the devil where I gained immortality but at the hidden cost of Hell on Earth. Frankly, I don't want to know what I would be capable of in fifty, a hundred more years. I'm ready, Sam. More than ready."

"If you're so sure, why'd you try to bribe Vick to recant his testimony?"

"I bribed the fella to come forward *against* me. He really needed the cash. You know what else?" Igor leaned forward and whispered as the deputy opened the door behind him. "I would've fucked the train station whore if I'd had a rubber. That's who I am, Bubba."

Sam pulled a photograph out of his back pocket and placed it in front of Igor on the table. "You know this dude?"

Igor picked up the selfie of Esau Jacobs. He looked quizzically at Sam. "Stay away from the goat that *used to be* in this photo," Igor said. "He's fuckin' crazy. It's sad, really."

"Sad?"

"Yeah, sad. He used to be an interesting guy. But that's what happens."

"What?"

"When we get too old."

Igor tossed the photo back on the table. It now depicted only an empty path through the woods.

CHAPTER FIFTEEN

DAY 6, MONDAY, OCTOBER 7, 2020

"At the conclusion of the case, you will see that the Commonwealth has failed to prove that Igor Alexi killed his wife, that he ever wanted her dead, or that he had any motive for committing the crime. Her death was a random act of terrible violence. We will ask you to find Igor not guilty."

Amelia finished her opening statement and sat down between Sam and Igor.

"Is the Commonwealth ready to proceed?" Judge Chan asked.

"The prosecution calls Clifford Vick."

The sixty-six-year-old international businessman strode past them to the witness stand. Sam focused intently on Vick's stride and facial expression. Calm. Confident. Sophisticated. Smooth. The same audition he had been on forever. It was an interesting decision for Sparf to call Vick first. The jury had not even heard about the killing yet. On the other hand, it was kind of smart to get Vick in and out fast and proactively portray Igor as a cold fish who had boasted about the brutal crime to a total stranger.

Chadwick Sparf approached the podium. Sam knew Sparf wanted to keep Vick's testimony simple and to the point—that a bitter Igor Alexi had spilled his guts to the sophisticated businessman, laying out details Vick could not otherwise have known. But Judge Chan, who would surely feel that substantial justice had been achieved if Igor Alexi were executed, was nevertheless evenhanded when it came to process. Vick was a jailhouse snitch in a death-penalty case. Sam would be allowed to ask him pretty much anything. Sam looked down at the banker's box next to him, neatly tabbed with the documents collected through Nguyen's investigation.

"State your name for the court, sir," Sparf said.

"Clifford Allen Vick."

"What do you do for a living?"

"I am the chief executive officer of Obelisk Enterprises, a financial consulting group headquartered in Washington, DC, and Cyprus."

"And briefly, sir, what does your company do?"

"Obelisk consults with corporations, usually foreign corporations, about various business interests in the United States."

A vague answer that meant exactly nothing.

"You're a lobbyist, then?" Sparf asked.

Vick appeared to ponder the question. "Sort of."

"Have you worked for the US government in the last five years?"

Vick paused as if to mull over his answer to be sure he spoke precisely. "Not directly."

"Are you under federal indictment for insider trading and money laundering?"

"Yes."

"Have you, in fact, pled guilty to those offenses?"

"Yes. I'll be sentenced in January."

"What is your understanding about what impact your testimony now, in this case, will have on your federal sentencing in January?"

"My understanding is that the government will inform my sentencing judge of my cooperation in this case."

"Have you been given any guarantees about what sentence you will receive?"

"Absolutely not. I'm facing a maximum penalty of forty years. My sentencing guidelines call for about fifteen years, because, I guess, of the amount of money involved." Vick glanced at the jury solemnly. The high-end grifter seemed honest.

"How do you know the defendant in this case, Igor Alexi?"

"I met Igor when I became his cellmate at the Bennet County Adult Detention Center for two days back in February of this year."

"Did you get along?"

"Sure, he seemed like a nice enough guy. We talked."

"Did you know what he was charged with?"

"Not at first. My lawyer had told me not to ask people in the jail about their charges. I'd never been to jail before, and he sort of gave me advice about how to act. He said to never be nosy about other people's business. So I just talked about regular stuff, sports or whatever. Igor likes hockey. Ovechkin. Capitals fan. I'm from Pittsburgh, so we talked about hockey."

Nodding slightly, Vick smiled up at Chan. Like one powerful person acknowledging another. With his dark suit and even, year-round tan, Vick was not a convict awaiting sentencing but an equal.

"Did Igor eventually talk about something other than hockey?"

"He talked about his kids," Vick said. "Irina, she's twenty-five, lives in LA, and Peter, he plays violin in the National Symphony. And the baby, Nataliya. She just started college in Pennsylvania. We talked about all kinds of stuff."

Amelia grimaced. The innocent details of Igor's life made it seem like Vick really knew their client. So typical. Such bullshit. The details of Igor Alexi's life were easy to discover. On the other hand, they were true.

"Did your conversations ever turn to his case?"

"Unfortunately, they did. He showed me a news article about it. Apparently, it was big news, but I hadn't heard about it. I was kind of preoccupied with my own problems while I was there. But, yeah, he showed me the article and then suddenly told me he was guilty. That he killed his wife."

"How did he say it?"

"First he talked about his charges. Said he had a trial coming up and that the prosecutor really didn't have anything. Then he suddenly blurted it out."

"What did he say exactly? About what he did?"

"He said, 'I'm glad I sliced her up. I would have screwed the *shluha* if I'd had a *preservatif.*' I know some Russian, and I double-checked later, when I got out. He said he would have screwed the whore if he'd had a condom."

"How did you react?"

"In the moment, I didn't react at all. But I told my lawyer about it later."

"Why? Why tell your lawyer about it?"

"I pretty much tell him everything, and frankly, it occurred to me that it might be valuable information that could help my case."

"At the time the defendant told you he killed his wife, were you working with the police?"

"No."

"Had anyone—your lawyer, a jail official, a prosecutor, or a cop—suggested to you that you could get a plea offer if you got Igor Alexi to confess?"

"Never. I'd never spoken to a single person about Igor until after he told me he did it. They can check my phone calls."

All inmate calls were recorded and available to the defense by subpoena. In fact, Nguyen had listened to every call, and, as Vick said, there was nothing.

"Is there any doubt in your mind that the defendant is the man who told you he killed his wife?"

"No, that's Igor."

"That's all the questions I have."

Sam leaned over to Igor, placed his hand on his back, and whispered, "We have to pretend to be talking about something right now. So, I'm gonna ask you one more time, Igor. Are you sure about this?"

Sam's hand could feel Igor's resolve.

"My soul used to run like the wind, Sam. I never want to be a crazy like Esau Jacobs."

Sam stood. "Judge, at this time Mr. Alexi wishes to change his plea to guilty. He wishes to waive his right to appeal and be sentenced to death today. Once you accept his plea, we will ask you to take up defense motion number IA-84, filed this morning, concerning methods of execution."

Sparf exchanged a glance with Judge Chan before both turned to look at Sam. Chan took a deep breath and glanced down at some papers in front of him. He said nothing, but motioned to the deputy, who quietly urged the jury to file out of the courtroom. Once they were gone, he leaned back in his seat and stared, softly, at Sam for a full thirty seconds.

"If that was a stunt to deliberately cause a mistrial, and Mr. Alexi is not actually ready to plead guilty, I'm going to hold you in contempt and jail you, Mr. Young."

Sam stood at the podium in silence.

"I'll accept your guilty plea if that's what you want to do, Mr. Alexi, but the ridiculous motion filed by your counsel—that the Commonwealth has only one chance to execute you—will be denied. The law is clear that no such exception applies, and that regardless of the methods of execution, if a death warrant is signed by the governor, you will be executed no matter how many tries it takes. I certainly hope you're not pleading guilty on that basis. You'd have a better chance with the jury. So, do you wish to plead guilty and waive any argument against this court's imposition of the death penalty, as your counsel just said?"

Igor stood, making eye contact with the judge. "Yes, Your Honor. I wish to be executed for my crime. But I'm afraid to tell you that as much as I wish this were not the case, the Commonwealth of Virginia will not be able to successfully execute me by lethal injection or electrocution, no matter how many times it tries."

Sam could hear the soft but rapid clicks of Lexi Shapiro's computer keys in the gallery behind him. He turned on his phone and the texts bounced through one after another. *Junk. Junk. Tawana.*

I need to see you, Samson. Tonight. You owe me one.

• • •

Sam, Amelia, and Nguyen remained at the counsel table long after the deputies took Igor away and the spectators had cleared out.

"The press will be out there," Amelia said as they gathered their trial materials into briefcases. "Are you going to say anything?"

Sam did not reply. Instead, he looked over at the prosecutor who was leaning back in his chair, arms folded, staring at the three of them.

"You people beat all," Sparf said. "If your guy was gonna do that, why didn't you take the deal? Shit, Sam, if you'd approached me even today, I'd have offered better. Didn't you just violate some defense lawyer code or something? Letting a guy agree to a death sentence?"

"Sometimes I don't know why," Sam said.

"I don't buy it," Sparf said. "You're planning something."

Sparf, clearly amused and relieved at his sudden victory, looked from one of them to the other, but his eyes rested on Nguyen. "I think you guys are planning to cut the tits off my fuck doll."

"That's a good one," Nguyen said.

"Then why didn't you object?" Sam said.

Sparf placed his thumb and index finger on his chin and glanced up at the ceiling, a gesture he often used when pondering something. Sam, Amelia, and Nguyen watched him think, as a deputy signaled that it was time for them to leave the courtroom.

"A murderer pled guilty," he finally said. Sparf picked up his briefcase, made a mock salute, and left.

"I'll see you guys back at the office," Nguyen said. "I've got a call to make."

"About this case?" Amelia asked.

"Sort of," Nguyen said. "I just figured out how we're gonna check in to the Hermon Hotel."

Sam saw the microphones and small semicircle of TV news reporters as soon as he opened the courthouse door and stepped into the sun. He approached them with Amelia.

"When Igor Alexi is sentenced, he will ask for the death penalty. However, even with his agreement, a death sentence would violate the Eighth Amendment's prohibition against cruel and unusual punishment, because Igor Alexi cannot be killed. Mr. Alexi is ninety-two years old and has been killed twice before, and yet here he is. Therefore, under the current state of the law, which gives Virginia an unlimited number of chances to kill him, his death sentence is not a death sentence at all but a sentence to eternity in prison—the first of its kind."

• • •

Sam took the stairs up to the office where Riker was playing solitaire on the coffee table in the reception area.

"How was court?" Riker asked.

"As if you don't know, Riker."

"Call me Lug Nut. And you've got a visitor. He's in your office."

"Why'd you let him into my office?"

"He seemed like the kind of guy who goes wherever he wants," Riker said. "And do I work here now or something?"

Sam walked past the reception area and approached his closed door. No, if the man from the phone was behind the door, he'd feel it. Sam opened the door.

Clifford Vick sat behind Sam's desk, in command of the small office he had never seen before. "Clearance for the private jet's not a problem," he said. "But the Hermon Hotel is gonna cost you."

CHAPTER SIXTEEN

NGUYEN CLICKED SOME KEYS on his computer. "Just checking the press action," he said to Sam.

"And?"

"It's hot, Bubba. A search for Igor Alexi has two full pages of hits. And here's you at the courthouse: 'Attorney Claims Convicted Murderer Not Human.'"

"What about credible news outlets?"

"Not sure who you consider credible, but everyone's running the AP story, and Shapiro's initial article is out. The point is, you're going viral."

"And the phone's ringing off the hook," Amelia said from the doorway. "Are we returning any of these?"

"Amelia, can you put together a press release?" Sam asked. "Attach Igor's DNA profile along with Camille Paradisi's and write it up. You know what to say. Both of them have impossible genetic profiles, blah-de-blah. And make sure the release has a photo of Camille from four years ago."

"Do you want to see it before I send it out?'

"No. Any of those press calls television?"

"Definitely." Amelia looked at her notes. "Local news stations seven and five. And CNN. That one's a New York number. Said they're doing a segment tonight."

"Call them. You're doing it."

"In New York?"

"They'll put you on camera in DC."

"To talk about what?"

Sam nodded to Nguyen, who stood. "Where we going?"

Sam walked into the conference room where he was suddenly surrounded by Riker, Esau, and to his surprise, Juliana and William. Amelia and Nguyen had followed.

"That was fast," Sam said to Juliana and William. "I would have understood if you couldn't make it."

"I told you it was damn interesting project," William said.

Sam regarded each individual in the room. *Slow time. Observe.* He walked towards the door with Nguyen close behind him.

"William, I'll meet you here tonight. Say, nine?" And to Juliana, "Do you have a suit?"

"Are we going to court?"

"You're going on TV with Amelia tonight. Tomorrow the rest of us are going skiing."

• • •

Nguyen drove the Escalade west on Interstate 66 while Sam gazed out the window.

"Where to, Bubba?"

"The Shangri-La."

"Yikes. Before that, can we discuss the travel plans?"

"Ready when you are."

"For Israel, I've got you, Amelia, Esau, Riker, Tawana, Camille. Who else is going?"

Sam did not reply.

Nguyen was hitting buttons on his phone. "Just texted you the wiring instructions from Vick. He's still using Steinberg's phone, by the way, just like I told you. But you're not gonna like it."

Sam opened Nguyen's text to reveal a message from Clifford Vick. "Looks good to me. He hooked us up." Nguyen turned onto the interstate towards the motel.

"The next text," Nguyen said,. "The one about his fee."

Sam clicked it open. "Whoa."

"Deal breaker?" Nguyen asked. They drove on in silence.

In the Shangri-La parking lot, Sam typed out a text.

"Use Vick's wiring instructions and send the fee from this account. You have to call to do it," Sam said.

"You're crazy, Bubba. I'll admit my idea to use Vick for the Hermon Hotel was brilliant. But he's a con artist. With this much cash, Vick'll glaze your donuts if you give him half a chance. What if we show up on the mountain and they've never heard of us? Where'd you get two million bucks? And, by the way, I need a raise."

"They'll ask you for a verbal password for the wire," Sam said. "I've never shared it with anyone."

Just then a gray sedan squealed into the parking spot two down from theirs. Sam's mind reached toward the car as the door opened.

"Shit, Nguyen, who's this? He's getting out."

A young man wearing sweatpants and a Nationals baseball cap quickly approached the Escalade.

"The Shangri-La?" he laughed. "With everything else going on, you guys decided to get your weasels greased?"

"You probably own the place," Nguyen said.

"Mr. Young." The man stuck out his hand. "Paulo Buterab. Just wanted to meet you."

Sam relaxed and shook the man's hand, who then returned to his car.

"Your mind's getting soft," Nguyen said. "You thought Paulo was fixin' to trim our hedges. You okay?"

Sam opened the door and stepped out, but turned back. "Me, you, Amelia, Tawana, Esau, Riker, Camille, okay?"

"Okay, Bubba."

• • •

Sam approached the motel and, for the second time that week, climbed the metal staircase to the second floor. *Slow time. Observe.* As he passed each door on the way to room 220, he reached beyond it and inside. He stepped around a drunk man sleeping in the walkway. Three doors before he reached Tawana's room, he felt her. Tawana was home, awake, alone, and knew he was coming. Her door opened when he stopped in front of it.

Tawana leaned lazily against the doorjamb, a provocative pose she probably used on clients, that is, if she was earning a living as a Shangri-La internet hooker. Sam attempted to probe just a bit into Tawana's mind but reeled back as though he had slammed into a locked steel door.

"Come in," Tawana said. "I was just about to call you."

Sam stepped into the room and Tawana blotted out the bright afternoon sun by softly closing the door. The drawn shades blocked just enough light to render the room dark and depressing. Sam noted the lack of clutter, clothes, or personal possessions on the bed, dresser, or small desk.

"How long have you been staying here?" He stopped and stood in front of the television as she took a seat on the edge of the bed. She wore a summer dress and sandals, roughly similar to the other outfits he'd seen her in. "Well?"

"Well, why are you moving forward with this foolishness? What's that Ukrainian trying to prove with this nonsense on television?"

"You know."

Instinctively, he reached again towards her mind and was met with a clang, like metal on metal.

"Stop, already," she said. Suddenly, deep wrinkles appeared around her eyes, disappeared, and appeared again. Her tears welled as her dark, smooth features were suddenly the face of an old woman. "You have no business doing what you're doing, Samson."

Tawana spoke in a low, cracking voice. She raised a wrinkled hand and ran it down the length of her suddenly gray hair as if for the first time. She slumped, seemingly melting into a soft, frumpy form on the corner of the bed. Sam reached towards her mind again and quickly pulled back. This time no barrier stopped him; he only flinched at what he felt there.

Just then an email buzzed in. eLocal.

"I'm not here alone," Sam said. He hit Nguyen's number.

"You've got your chink in one car and a gypsy with a gun in the other. I'm not scared of guns, Samson. Or chinks or gypsies." Tawana's guttural voice rose. She stood, youthful and beautiful again.

Sam stepped back and reflexively reached out to Tawana with his mind again and sailed right in, as if invited. He was too late to get away. She was too close, the space too confined. And he was, after all, just a person. Her mind was two steps past snapping his neck. She took a step towards him.

His phone flew out of his hand and across the room, rattling into the corner and bouncing with a thud on the thin carpet. Before he could take a step toward the door, it opened and shut quickly as light briefly played over the room and a streak passed in front of him.

A wet, sickening thud. Blood spurted from Tawana's face. Her body seemed to leap onto the bed, where it writhed for a few seconds as blood pooled around her head. Then she stopped moving. A large knife protruded from her right eye socket, buried to the hilt.

Camille Paradisi stood next to him, arms folded, a suburban jogger in shorts and T-shirt, fanny pack and all. She quickly opened the pack and then dragged Tawana off the bed and across the room towards the far window, where she wrestled with the lifeless body for several seconds. When Camille stood, Tawana was hog-tied with two sets of metal handcuffs. Her right hand was fastened to the radiator with a third set. Camille stood and glanced at Sam before walking into the bathroom. Sam listened to her washing her hands.

"All she could think to do to stop us was to kill you," Camille said over her shoulder.

Sam collected his phone from the corner without speaking. Before opening the door, they both looked back at Tawana.

"When're we leaving?" Camille asked.

"You must already know that. Tomorrow."

Sam and Camille calmly passed the other rooms along the walkway—drunk man still sleeping—and then descended the metal staircase.

"She really was going to kill you just then," Camille said, as if to drive home the point that her actions had been justified. Sam remembered, from four years ago, that she had always seemed to care what he thought of her.

"Okay."

The Escalade's motor turned over as they approached. Then the gray sedan's.

This was probably the only time he and Camille would ever discuss Tawana Salome Ortiz Hightower from Buenos Aires. "Salome can't catch a break with this family, can she?"

Camille did not reply.

Sam opened the door to the Escalade, but Camille touched his shoulder. "One more stop. Come with me, Sam. Please."

"Looking good, Camille," Nguyen said. "Long time no see."

Sam looked at his phone and clicked the eLocal message. *No hard feelings, Samson, but I'm gonna live forever. Salome.*

"I'll meet you back at the office," he said to Nguyen.

"I need that verbal password, Sam," Nguyen said.

"The password is 'Fifika's son,'" Camille said.

Sam clicked *claim lead.*

CHAPTER SEVENTEEN

CAMILLE OPENED THE TRUNK of her Hyundai rental and fished around while Sam gazed across Route 1. He checked his phone. *8:20 p.m.* Camille, now carrying a small backpack over her shoulder, gently shut the trunk.

"Are you about ready to tell me what we're doing?" Sam asked.

Camille fixed her eyes on his and then looked past him, across the road and down a steep hill. "You didn't think I'd miss my brother's funeral, did you? You think I lack all sentimentality?"

"Sometimes," Sam said.

"Feelings were always Fifika's thing. Unfortunately. For her, that is."

"The service is on Saturday."

"The funeral is right now, Bubba. Follow me."

Sam and Camille crossed Route 1, descended some stairs, and walked into the dark, out of view of the busy road, towards what Sam could now see was a small cemetery. Camile slowed her pace as they entered through a low black metal gate. The enclosed graveyard was larger than it had first appeared, winding behind a stand of evergreen trees and concealed from the road.

Camille stopped in front of a simple grave marker, a gray stone cross, and set her backpack on the ground.

The marker read *Alifair Rajo 1935–2000.* "Who was she?" Sam asked. "Family? Related to our Alifair? Related to us?"

"She was a good soul who had a hard life."

Camille removed a square metal tin and a foldable camping shovel from her backpack.

"You stole Paul's ashes?" Sam asked.

"I'd hardly call it stealing." She placed the tin on the ground and stood erect, holding the shovel.

"I don't like to think about what we did to this man," Camille said.

Sam watched her closely in the dim light. He could hear cars whizzing by not far from the other side of the grove of trees. He wondered if she would cry, if speaking about her brother like this would engender a standard human emotion.

"He never got to be normal. Born into a family with me and Fifika. The first half of his life was with her and the second with me. And he never got to be whatever he wanted. He was a drug dealer, a pimp, a priest. Who really wants to be any of those things? He was beautiful and kind and so . . . human. Fika should've left him behind way back then. He probably could have been a shopkeeper or maybe the best-looking schoolteacher in Bariloche. But no, Fifika and her sentimentality. She dragged him through the life of one of us, but he wasn't one of us. And all the while she pretended she did it for him. At least our mother knew to leave town alone. Resurrected ones never linger, right?"

The last four years had proven that the never-linger principle certainly applied to Camille with her own daughter.

Camille unfolded the small shovel and handed it to Sam.

"Alifair, whoever she is, is already buried here," Sam whispered.

"No," Camille said. "She's not."

Sam broke the ground and found it rockless and soft under the grass. He dug a hole about a two feet deep while Camille stood quietly. When he finished, Camille placed the tin in the hole and Sam filled it. Camille then reached into her backpack and removed a thin wooden placard. She tore a thick adhesive strip from the back and gently placed the placard over Alifair Roja's name.

"I'll do better if I can ever come back," she said.

If?

Paul Tomas Kritalsh. 1947–2019. He Was Strong Inside.

"Who was Alifair?"

Camille shouldered her backpack and started to walk towards the road, but she turned back with a grim but triumphant smile, like a soldier who has realized she barely survived a battle when others had not. She looked so calm and beautiful and young, like a magazine cover girl on a hike who everyone wanted either to be or be with.

"What must it have been like for him?" she asked. "Being normal and being with us?"

Sam could venture a guess but instead said, "I want to know the rest."

They walked back to the car together. They stayed quiet as she pulled onto Route 1 towards downtown. He checked his watch.

"You have to understand, I was so much more in tune with who we were, and at such a younger age than Fifika," she said. "I laugh a little when I read her journal, casting me way back to when I was some kind of smiling prankster dancing and singing around the shack. But it wasn't like that. I knew what I was, not everything, but enough. And I knew she was, and our mother, too.

But I left my sister in the hands of a rapist and our crazy mother, magic though she was. So funny how even we turn out so different from each other. That our mother, one of us, would still be slave to a man? But when I found Fifika again, I knew right away she was different than me. She worried like a regular person, and it drove her crazy. I watched you grow up from a distance, and she gave raising you her best try—the regular life with you and her studies and all of that. I'm not sure she really believed who she was until she found herself alive on the deck of a ship in the Atlantic Ocean after being underwater for ten hours in a crashed plane. Then she knew. Knew for sure that I'd been right all along."

"Why didn't she come back?" Sam asked. "After the plane crash? At least explain things to me? Resurrected ones never linger, is that it? They just abandon everybody?"

Camille was quiet for a moment. He thought she was either unsure of the answer or, more likely, unwilling to infuse the moment with the truth.

"My mother died, her first time at least, in 2000," Sam said. "The same year as Alifair Roja."

"She did," Camille said. "Just a few days apart."

Sam took out his phone and did an internet search, and then another, while Camille pulled into one of the parking spots in in the empty strip in front of Sam's office. *Vlax Romani. Vlax Romani to English.*

Camille turned off the car and looked at Sam. He remembered now, from four years ago, how she was sometimes like this. She played his game, in a way. Letting silences sit so others would fill them—sometimes with information they should have kept to themselves. But Camille's silences were more than that. They were attempts to communicate complex thoughts with looks. When she did answer, her words were often a response not to the question someone had asked, but rather to the question they should have asked.

"Alifair Roja was not your mom," Camille said. Sam did a search on his phone. *I-translate. Vlax Romani to English. Roja = Heaven. Alifair = Heaven. Camille Paradisi.*

"Who was she, then?"

"I haven't seen Fifika in over two years." Camille's voice uncharacteristically cracked with emotion. "I don't know where she is. I thought that if I were around you I could get a read on her, even if she were far away—like I could years ago, when we were young. But she's shutting me out on purpose. She always said she would never tolerate me bringing you into this, into any of it. She wanted everything normal for you. She never understood that it couldn't be that way. I tried to meet you when you were younger. On the day of your high school graduation, I told her I was going to introduce myself to you as her friend. That I was going to try to start a relationship with you. To tell you everything. We argued over it, and she won. Obviously, four years ago I brought you into it anyway. I thought I'd convinced her that you could help us and you'd be fine, which I still believe."

Camille was now crying. A real cry, like one might hear from an actual, lonely mother who had lost her sister, buried her brother, and abandoned her child. The two sat in silence, the silence like a tug of war over whether Camille would answer Sam's question about Alifair Roja. But who Alifair Roja had been hardly mattered. Sam decided to ask something that did.

"Are you gonna go see our Alifair? Your daughter. Alifair Andrada."

"Alifair Roja didn't just die in 2000," Camille said. "Your mother killed her. She was me."

CHAPTER EIGHTEEN

SAM SAT IN HIS office with William while outside the open door, Nguyen bustled back and forth down the hall on the phone.

"Our initial attempt to sequence Lugnudsky failed," William said. "The process views him as an incomplete profile. He has only one set of genes, and at our sensitivity level the system thinks his single alleles at a locus—in his case at all loci—mean the sample is corrupted. In other words, the process thinks it's being asked to sequence an incomplete profile, not the complete profile of someone with only one inherited allele at each locus. We're working on it. This was our first rushed effort."

"Did you see CNN?" Sam said.

William nodded. "They're on the way back. They did great. Amelia laid out the legal issue. As far as I understand it, if Igor Alexi can't die, that somehow means the death sentence is illegal. Juliana explained the impossibility of Paradisi and Alexi being homozygotic at all the forensic loci. The odds of it occurring in a human. And Paradisi's mysterious disappearance four years ago. They touched all the bases. The host was incredulous."

"Did Juliana say she was working on sequencing their entire genomes? Did she say we had *more* than just two profiles?"

"She didn't. The genome part can't be public yet. We're flying under the radar at the school. And she didn't feel comfortable outing people whose DNA she hadn't typed."

"Thanks, William. Feeling okay?"

"I am. I have to say, this project has been damn therapeutic. Full disclosure, Sam. These discoveries could win us, meaning myself and Julianna, the Nobel Prize. I sent you an email about an hour ago. Just some thoughts on the genealogy stuff we talked about. Basically—and I don't know, and am not asking, where you are headed with all this—but if it matters, there's a real chance your alien gene entered the Kritalsh bloodline pretty recently. I thought you may want to keep that in mind because, well—"

"That would mean a real alien could still be around. Thanks, William. I get it." Sam checked his phone. "Make yourself at home." He left his office and walked quickly towards the kitchen where he opened the freezer. He poured four fingers of cold vodka into a coffee mug.

"One more thing, Sam," William said, following him into the kitchen. He held out a plain, sealed envelope labeled simply *Sam*. "Your forensic typing results. Your chart. Not the whole genome, just the basic forensic work. You know how to read them. For what you're looking for, anyway."

Sam took the envelope, folded it, and tucked it into his back pocket.

Nguyen rounded the corner. "All set, seven-twenty p.m. departure tomorrow."

Sam sipped from his mug. "Details?"

"Sending them out now. Meet at Reagan at five, General Aviation Terminal."

"Private flight?" Sam said. "You sure that's a good move?"

"It's all set up," Nguyen said. "Land in Haifa at seven-ten a.m. Then a chartered bus to, well, that's kind of up to you."

"I don't know, Nguyen. Private pilots? It could be anybody, and—"

"Don't worry about it, Bubba. Our pilot isn't just anyone. We're flying on Barnabus Farley's jet."

Sam smiled. "And Mount Hermon?"

"We're a group of tourists trying to summit the highest mountain in as many countries as we can. Vick thought of that. He got us special permission from the UN facility. The dude is not that dumb."

"I bet."

• • •

Sam stood on his roof, drink in hand, gazing across the city. The ritual, drinking alone in precisely the same spot almost every night, had been—sadly—part of his life for four years. Even longer really, with the view from the top of a mansion he had never earned more of a recent addition. He usually worked sporadically during the ritual. Phone calls. Sudden ideas about a case. He bounced between his perch by the rail and his laptop in the kitchen at the bottom of the spiral staircase. One way or another, the ritual was over. His phone buzzed.

"Hey, William."

"Just wanted to run a few more things by you, before, you know, the trip." William sounded so tired.

"Hi, Sam," Juliana said in the background.

"She's a veritable star now," William said. "Although her supervisor at work is a little baffled by the whole thing. But I know you've got a lot to deal with right now, so I'll talk you through my thoughts, okay?"

"Please." Sam drained his glass and poured another while listening to William through the speakerphone.

"We've talked about the fact that your demon gene is unlikely to have survived since ancient times. One important thing to note about the recessive model is that once a second-generation half-breed starts mating with humans, the chances of the demon gene surviving decrease with each generation. And you're talking a lot of generations."

"I remember this Mendelian stuff from high school."

"What I'm trying to say is that maybe the demon gene is dominant in the first generation—coming from a purebred parent— and recessive from then on. That matches with the Bible story, right? Under that theory, either there were two purebred demons romancing southern Argentina, or—"

"Or one, who knocked up Great Grandma *and*, years later, Grandma Kritalsh," Sam said.

"Or that, yeah."

Sam touched his back pocket and felt the outline of William's envelope containing his own forensic profile. "What does all of this mean for me?"

"Using the demon gene model—presuming your mother carried it—if the gene is recessive, then you still can't manifest it unless your father carried it, manifested or not. If your father did carry it, you have a twenty-five-percent chance of manifesting it. If your father did not carry it, then you have a twenty-five-percent chance of carrying it, unmanifested. Manifested or not, if you carry it, you can pass it down, but none of your offspring will manifest it unless you breed with someone carrying it . . . You open your envelope yet?"

"Do you know what it shows?"

"No, I did it blind. A lab tech knows, but not your name. It's just for you."

"Thanks for everything, William. I've got one more question. Wasn't Jesus born by virgin birth? Not by sex with a god?"

"Good thought," William said. "Virgin birth is first discussed in the book of Isaiah, and the Hebrew word used is *almah,* which means young woman. Almah can mean virgin because young unmarried women in that culture were assumed to be virgins, but the word itself does not imply anything about chastity. The word is used seven times in the Hebrew Bible, and none of these instances suggests it was meant to imply virginity. Second, the term *virgin,* in any language, means someone who has not had sex with another person."

"I get it," Sam said. "Our hybrids aren't people."

"I have one final, final question for you, Sam."

The doorbell rang. Nothing about it made Sam afraid, exactly, despite the fact that doorbells ringing this late at night in this kind of neighborhood happen only for a bad reason. Like the cops. Sam reached his mind downstairs and towards the locked front door, but felt nothing. He took the stairs out of the kitchen, mind now intently focused, reaching and reaching through the painted wooden door, and almost forgetting William on the phone.

"What's the question?" Sam said.

"What do you actually know about your father?"

"I'll talk to you soon, William," Sam said, hanging up. He placed his hand on the doorknob and tried to reach through it with his mind again. *Nothing.*

Sam opened the door. He heard the first two shots before realizing they carried a menacing import. By the time the last shot followed the first two into his chest and he fell back, he knew he was being killed by Esau Jacobs. He just had time to notice the smell before it was over. It was the grizzly bear smell surrounding those filled with hate. He suddenly recalled a thought from long ago, maybe from a class, or a TV show, about the definition of nothing. That people imagined that *nothing* was a black void. But empty black space was something. Nothing, as Aristotle more properly defined it, was what rocks dream of. Sam waited, able to feel blood oozing around him, for a nothing that never came. And then he thought of Igor, and the stag.

My soul runs with the wind.

CHAPTER NINETEEN

WHEN SAM CAME TO, he found himself sitting across the street from his house, on a bench in front of the D-Day Memorial. Every time he ventured downstairs, across the street, and down the hill to the bench for a closer look at the monument, he noticed something new about it. This time, he noted that one of the men, the one positioned to be third out of the Higgins Boat, gazed upwards rather than fiercely ahead like the other men. *Did the artist intend a meaning there? A suggestion that someone or something above was apt to take sides? To favor this man over the enemies firing on them from the beach? Or the mere, maybe even irrational, hope that such a being existed?*

"You've gotta relax your mind, Samson."

Sam turned with a start to see Camille on the bench next to him. Again, she wore shorts, a T-shirt—Catholic University this time—and running shoes, as if out for an evening jog.

"Slow time, observe—remember?" she said. "You never

should've let that skinny old buzzard creep up on you that easily. You're distracted."

Sam, staring blankly down the hill, did not reply at first, but his mind felt at peace, at rest.

"You know," he said, "some people think women shouldn't jog alone at night around here. You could get sexually assaulted. Killed even. A few years ago a serial killer stalked these parts."

"Do tell," she said. "One of the bodies was found just over there, from what I recall." Camille looked down the slightly sloping hill towards the Netherlands Bell Tower. "If I run across any women, I'll pass your warning along. I got you some water."

Sam regarded Camille closely and then glanced at his phone, which somehow lay next to him on the bench. He reached for it. It was sticky with what could have been something like syrup but was, of course, dried blood. *3:20 a.m.*

Camille nodded towards a red plastic cup sitting next to Sam on the bench. He drained it and tossed the cup towards a trash receptacle behind them. It glanced off the rim and then skittered across the ground behind Camille. The cup came to rest but then leapt into the air and whisked itself into the bin, ringing against the inside with a faint metallic *ting*.

"Is that a new thing?" he asked.

"Working on it."

"So, did you know? About me?" Sam asked.

"I thought I did. I usually do, but I wasn't sure until now. I think it was hard to see for sure, because, you know—"

"We're related."

"Yeah, I've known Jacobs for years. We call him PFC Williamson. He was lurking around, so I around, so I was keeping an eye on him, kind of from a distance. He shot you with that old pistol he totes around from the Civil War. I was just pulling up when he did it, and he buggered off fast down the street. He was limping, as always, but he still moves so fast it's like his hair's on fire. I thought about going after him, but instead I pulled you inside and shut the door in case somebody called the cops."

"And?"

"Those little guns are pretty quiet. Low-velocity ammunition. And the houses are so big, I guess nobody thought the little bangs were gunshots. That gun is barely bigger than his hand."

Sam felt his chest again; stickiness, and a large hole in his shirt, but no injury.

"Why do this? Is it so bad? Living forever? Learning more and more about yourself? What about all the possibilities? All the good you could do? That we could do? The adventure even?" Sam recognized the energy and excitement in his own voice.

Camille stared straight ahead but did not reply for a long moment.

"My stepfather's friend, Victorio it was, used to pay him to have sex with me. He wasn't the only one. I didn't know any better, like maybe it was a normal part of life, and frankly I preferred Victorio and most of the others to Miguel. But I still left home at fifteen, leaving my sister in the hands of this pimp rapist who somehow had my mother's heart. To survive, I sold myself for money like a slave. I thought I was crazy and evil and every terrible thing you could imagine. Finally, I jumped in front of a speeding truck in the middle of the night outside Caracas. The truck didn't even stop, but I came to on the side of the road what must have been a few hours later." She didn't sound sad, horrified, or boastful.

"One morning that summer, I pulled a knife on a man after he fucked me under a bridge. I did it because I knew he had a gun and hoped he would shoot me dead. The coward pulled out his gun but held it awkwardly with his trembling hand—a grown man with a gun, scared of a young girl with a knife. I snatched the gun from his hand, put it against my head, and fired. When I woke up the man was gone, and the gun was on the ground by me. The fool had run off without his gun."

She turned to look at Sam.

"Every time I robbed or killed with that gun, I hated the victims for getting to die. What you don't understand yet is that none of it, the adventure, as you put it, means anything unless there's an end. A life like this is hell. I don't hate life, Sam. I just hate being like this. And we don't age well, despite how it looks. My mother was batshit crazy by the time she had us. And look at Esau. He's full of power, but his mind's shot. He hates the world and himself, lives like a pig, and he can never die. He's shot himself with that little pistol before, too. This, Sam, is our future."

Camille smiled. "Sorry to be so intense. As far as all the good I could do if I lived forever, that's probably more your thing. Your legal fee for this gig ought to be quite the springboard if you wanna get into the do-gooder business, Samson Young."

"I thought I was already in the do-gooder business. I took the case and I'm gonna finish it, but not for the money."

"Oh really? Maybe we should donate your legal fee to Habitat for Humanity. Twenty-four million buys a lot of homes for hillbillies, right? Maybe your friend Esau will get one."

With a nod, Camille directed Sam's attention to the monument in front of them. The third charging man in line, now grimacing, stared ahead towards the unseen enemy, having apparently abandoned his hope for immortal favor and decided to go it alone. Camille placed her arm over Sam's shoulder.

"Most of the people clinging so hard to life are dead already," she said.

"You sure you need me for this?" Sam asked.

Camille did not answer right away but held an unfocused stare past the memorial and down the hill, towards nothing.

"People should stay with their kind."

Sam thought about Igor again.

My soul runs like the wind.

CHAPTER TWENTY

DAY 7, TUESDAY, OCTOBER 8, 2019

"You got a meeting, Bubba," Nguyen said. He and Amelia sat in the client chairs in Sam's office. "Riker wants to see you. He seems a little confused. About the plan."

"What are you gonna do until the flight?" Sam asked.

"Shit, boss, I know I don't have much of a life, but I got a few things to do this afternoon. I've never flown out of the country without a return trip booked. It's a little, well, asshole-clenching. And I gotta finish up the arrangements with Vick. He's making me meet him at some fancy office in DC. It's kinda funny. I spend six months preparing to lube his chassis, and now we're pals. He's trying to hire me, FYI. But don't worry, I told him I'm committed to your fanatical religious mission. At least for now."

"I'm still working on the research we talked about," Amelia said. "So, I'm headed home. But I got a question. I didn't grow up with this religion stuff, so, sorry if I'm being dense, but this whole virgin-birth thing . . . did the angel knock her up?"

"Huh. I've never heard anyone say that before."

"I'm just sayin'. The Bible says he came into her. There's some stuff out there about it. That's not it?"

"No one's ever just sayin'."

• • •

Riker sat at the bar at Harpoon Hannah's, drinking a glass of ice water and scrolling through his phone.

Sam placed his bag on the ground and took the barstool next to Riker. "You hang out here?" The bartender placed a cold vodka in front of him. "No, thanks, Sarah. Club soda."

Sarah gave him an odd look. "I like your friend."

"Never been here," Riker said without glancing towards Sarah. "I picked it 'cause you hang here. I don't even drink." He paused until Sarah left to serve another customer.

"I really appreciate you guys helping out with my case, and I guess I'm even glad you let me know that I'm, well, special or whatever you want to call it. But I don't need to know all about this stuff. I always knew I was unusual. And this is gonna sound stupid, but I just thought I had an intense form of ADHD or something. One time in sixth grade, our teacher explained that the reason we'd had a substitute teacher for three days was that she'd had the flu. We'd missed a field trip, which pissed off the class. And exactly when she said it, I knew, just like that, that she was lying. She'd travelled out of town with her boyfriend. I even knew their destination—New York City—a place I had only a vague conception of."

Riker took a sip of water and dabbled a finger in the wet spot it had left on the bar.

"At the end of the day, thinking I was being cute, I went up to her and asked her how she enjoyed her trip to New York. Her face changed immediately, and she looked at me with such ferocity I realized I'd done something terribly wrong. The next day, I was in the principal's office, answering questions about whether I was stalking Ms. Dworkin or whatever. I learned then to keep my thoughts to myself. Nobody likes a know-it-all. And as time went on I tried to suppress it, my strangeness. I never tried to excel in school, though I could have, or at life. I'm a freakin' flower delivery guy. But really, its okay."

Sam didn't have to push his mind toward Riker to sense where this was going.

"I've been talking to your other client, Tawana. I'm not going with you on your trip. No hard feelings either way. But I do have a question. What am I? You must know more than I do, or you wouldn't be doing all this."

Sam regarded Riker, who had yesterday oozed with the sincerity of a nervous client but now glowed with the confidence of a man in command, and demanding answers. But did he fear new information about himself? Sam couldn't fathom how a guy like Riker must feel about the whole endeavor. Like a patient waiting for a potentially life-altering diagnosis, or an athlete about to snatch a victory he had never imagined. In asking the question, Riker had more guts than he himself had displayed when faced with the same question. And while Sam had been too afraid of his own identity to demand the answer, he had outed Riker—to Riker himself, as well as to others—without Riker's permission.

"You'll have to figure it out for yourself, Lug Nut."

Sarah leaned over the bar to speak softly to Riker. Anyone could see the young bartender was trying to make a friend. They spoke quietly for a moment, until Sarah smiled at him and then glanced, a little nervously, at Sam as she glided down the bar.

"Just the facts, ma'am," Riker said to Sam, winking. He affectionately touched Sam's shoulder, stood and began to leave, but turned for one more comment, this one to Sarah.

"I'll see you at closin' time, darlin'."

• • •

"Back in ten minutes," Sam said to the Uber driver, who had just eased into the parking spot directly in front of Andrada's residence on the Holy Angels property. Andrada's truck still occupied the same space it had the night Sam found his body.

Anna Buterab opened the door, and Alifair ran to Sam and hugged him. She did not speak just then, nor when he sat with her on the couch. Sam sought meaning in her silence—a wisdom beyond her years, or just muteness born of one tragedy after another in such an odd, young life.

"I'm going away for a while," Sam said. "Maybe just a few days, maybe a little longer. But after that, I want you to come live with me, in my house. Forever."

Alifair kept squeezing him, but her eyes darted to Anna.

"Anna, too," Sam said. "If she'll take the job. I have a big house. And Anna's gonna need a raise. Nothing Uncle Steve needs to know about." Sam winked at Anna, who smiled and placed her hand on Alifair's head.

"Is that okay with you, Alifair?"

Sam eased back into the Uber.

"Airport," he said. He did a quick Google search. Second Circuit Court of Appeals. His call bounced between secretaries, with long holds in between.

"Hey, man, to what in the universe do I owe this honor?"

"Yeah, whatever, Marvin. You're a fancy-pants attorney now, and you know it. Have you applied for your Supreme Court clerkship yet?"

"It's pending, Sam. And if I didn't think you actually knew my name was Melvin, I'd kick your ass."

"Glad all is well. You get my text?"

"Typical Sam Young message. No explanation. I'm supposed to figure it out on my own."

"Did you?"

"You know I did. You wouldn't think I'd recognize a voice from a ten-minute interaction four years ago. But I did. It's the guy."

"How would you explain it? How did you recognize the voice?"

"It's not the voice, exactly. More of a combination of the tone and the accent. The guy speaks with a commanding whisper, each word polished like the stones in a stream. And the accent—this may sound weird, but it's like an averaging out of all the accents in the world. I have no doubt it's the dude who stopped me at the pier in Buenos Aires. The old guy who was carrying around a fifty-year-old itinerary like he knew I was coming. That part's always kind of freaked me out. Also, Sam, I'd been thinking about this before you texted, and there's something I never told you about that guy."

"Why not?"

"Because it's not believable, and not really relevant. Hearing his voice brought it back to me."

"All good. What is it?"

"Yeah, sure, actually—hold on."

Melvin came back in a moment.

"Just wanted to shut my door. So, shortly after I walked away from the old man—after he let me take a photograph of the itinerary and everything—I went back. I felt like I should have asked him more questions, even some basics like who was he, how did he know so much from so long ago, stuff like that. I wanted to do a good job. So, I go back to the deck about thirty minutes later and the dude is, of course, gone. But a cop, like some kind of Port Authority policeman, approached me and demanded an ID. And he's speaking Spanish really fast, and I begin to realize he's suspicious of me. He asks me if I'm on drugs, or drunk, if I've ever been committed to a mental hospital, and then another cop joins him and it starts getting scary, like, what the hell do these guys think I did, or are they suspicious of me for asking all over about Salome and trying to make an excuse to detain me. Finally they ask me to step into their office, which is pretty much right there, just a small, nondescript building. Of course, I have to follow them. I'm in a foreign country and don't know the rules. So, they sit me down and play me a video clip. I guess the whole port is under camera surveillance, which makes sense, and it's a video clip of when I was talking to the guy."

Melvin stopped talking for a second.

"And?"

"And the video clip showed me in a five-minute conversation with no one. The guy wasn't there at all. I was gesturing, talking, and taking photos, with no one. Remember when I asked you on the phone if you wanted to see the photo of me with the guy, and you said no? Well, after a few minutes with the cops, they seemed to realize I wasn't crazy or drunk or on drugs, and I made something up about practicing for a role in a play. They laughed it off and let me go. So, I'm walking away and I realize, shit, *I* took a picture of me with the guy. I look at my phone, and there he is with my arm around him, smiling in the bright sun with his skin like the hide on a football. I'm thinking, who knows what these cops were up to? Their video system is messed up. So I forgot about it."

"Okay, I hear you. Weird stuff happens."

"That's not it. When I got your text earlier, I looked back on my phone— my photos are stored in the Cloud—and I pull it up."

"I'd like to have it now," Sam said.

"No problem, but here's the thing. That guy Van Zyl's not in it anymore. It's me with my arm around nothing."

CHAPTER TWENTY-ONE

DAY 8, WEDNESDAY, OCTOBER 9, 2019,
MOUNT HERMON, ISRAEL-SYRIA BORDER

Sam's eyes opened. He lay in bed, staring at the ceiling and marveling for a moment at his inner sense of levity, an almost physical bliss, like a deep feeling of calm as his body and mind awakened. He began to think about the day ahead. Then he suddenly understood the feeling. For the first time in years, his first waking moment was utterly unimpaired by a hangover.

He turned towards the clock on the nightstand and saw an envelope next to him on the bed. It had not been there the afternoon before, just after he checked into his room at the Vintage Holiday Village and Spa. He held up the envelope and saw that it had no name on it. But he nevertheless knew it contained a letter for him, from her. And he also knew that she was here, at the base of Mount Hermon, joining them after all.

Dear Samson,

I knew right away your father was from Africa, Dutch, Afrikaners as they say, after only a moment around him. But back then I couldn't have imagined the truth. When I look back across the years to the first few moments we spent together— along with Paul, on the deck of La Liberacion *the day we left Argentina forever—his absence is a wound that never heals.*

Years later, he's still in my dreams, and then he appears and changes my life for the second time because after that I had you. I suppose I betrayed you in the end. Maybe, though, there's an upside to all the time people like us have here. More chances to get it right.

When I first read about the enlightened monks from the olden times, the ones our modern days no longer produce, I knew that the yogis who made it so close to enlightenment they could see it, could touch it, were my kindred spirits, my brothers and cousins. Yours too. You have so much to learn.

When the soul leaves the body, we can actually meet, speak with, touch, even have sex with others who are consciously projecting just then. Once you're good, those people can be across the world. Once you're great, those people can be dead. But at these times of deep meditation, most of the people you run across are merely sleeping. Their souls are out of their bodies, but unconsciously so. Perhaps you can interact with them a bit—maybe they'll remember you in a dream—but that's more like chatting with someone who's half asleep or sedated. In any event, that's how it starts, gazing dreamily around at zombies, and looking down at your own physical body sitting still below. And my soul is in the sky, just as Shakespeare said. A book I once read, a Theravadin text, suggested that to be caught—to awaken—while your soul is in the sky would result in death. Your soul failing to return on time, if you will, to your body. But that's not true. Our souls can fly, like light, from anywhere at all to arrive just in time. Ever notice the brief feeling of falling when you suddenly awake from deep sleep? Someday you will be able to see more of the past, most of the present, and some of the future. Eventually, maybe, too much.

This morning I will be perched on the corner of my bed, just a floor below you, and my soul will be in the sky. I will hear a knock at the door and fly, like light, back into my body in time to hear the second knock. I will open the door.

"Hello, Marcela." Your father will call me by my American name.

"Hello, Johannes."

We will walk together through the hotel lobby in our long black jackets like a couple who knows each other's strides. How will we appear? Like ex-lovers? Like a father and daughter? Or something else? But there will be no guests to ponder us, no one at all in sight until we ease through the revolving door, me first, out of the hotel, into the cool air, and I will see you. You with Raj, your friends, and with Camille.

You will look alive and unafraid, and so young, no older than my sister. You won't say anything at first. You'll only glance at Camille. I'll hug Raj first, nod towards Camille, and then step in front of you. I will sense Johannes behind me, and in Camille's eyes flickering past me towards him, I'll see their recent acquaintance quite clearly. Then I'll speak to you.

"Trinity was right. That you could get us here if you tried." You will frown, skeptical, and you'll push your mind towards me and I won't resist. And then you'll see that I have been in your dreams.

We'll ride in two Jeeps, each with a middle-aged driver in green fatigues and a blue beret. You and your friends will ride together in the lead Jeep, and I'll see you talking with each other as the Jeeps head up and up into the treeless hills.

Soon we'll be standing in a group in front of a concrete military installation, you in front, as a tall Black man approaches us. Colonel Guy, he'll say. A Caribbean man who speaks like it, that pretty lilt. One hour at the summit. Not a moment longer.

Soldiers will pat us down for weapons before leading us through a gate. We'll follow Colonel Guy, one of us in front of the other.

A young Irish soldier will walk with us a bit further. O'Donald.

"Just over this hill, briefly into the valley between, then up that snowy ridge. Pretty easy, really," O'Donald will say.

We'll walk single file: You, Camille, Amelia, Nguyen, Barnabus, Raj, me, Johannes. Less than a mile, and we'll be standing in a half circle, gazing into Syria. 11:55 local time.

We'll stand silently for what feels like quite a while.

"This is a seriously fucked up situation," you'll say.

And yeah, Samson. I'll give you that.

"You know what else?"

"Yeah," Amelia will say. "Vick didn't pay anybody that two million dollars."

And we'll wait, the eight of us, without speaking, as the minutes click by. Five, then twenty.

"This is bullshit," Barnabus will say from behind me. He'll raise his hands, middle fingers extended, and scream across the empty view, "Who the fuck do you think you are? Where are you shitbirds?"

"Colonel what's-his-name's gonna send for us soon," Amelia will say.

And suddenly he will be among us. Be very careful, Samson. I'll be there with you.

CHAPTER TWENTY-TWO

NGUYEN NODDED ACROSS THE snow. "We've got company." A UN solider approached alone, her dark fatigues starkly contrasting with the snow and the open blue sky behind her.

The woman's eyes remained fixed on the ground as she neared the group. In a moment, she stood in front of them, a small smile on her face, as if their presence provided mild amusement, a break in what might have normally been a pretty boring job manning a mountaintop outpost. She was probably about twenty-five and maybe even younger. Under her crisp, new-looking beret, her head was shaved perfectly clean, with no stubble or tan lines, as if it had always been that way. As the UN soldiers seemed to represent a smorgasbord of nationalities—anything but American—Sam pegged her as maybe South American or Spanish. Or was it Middle Eastern or Indian? *What life choices would bring someone like her to an outpost like this?* he thought. Whatever her heritage, she spoke plain American English.

"Shitbirds, Mr. Farley? Your time's almost up. You get what you need, Samson?"

"No."

"Too bad. But hey, how about a group photo? Summiting Mount Hermon, right?" She reached out and Sam limply handed over his phone. The eight of them formed a line, arms around each other, Sam in the middle, between his aunt and his mother, with Van Zyl on his mother's right between her and Raj, and the others to Camille's left.

"Great view." The woman clicked a series of shots before handing the phone back to Sam. "Time to get on back to the base, I guess."

The woman turned and started to walk away. Sam examined the photo, and as he focused on one and then the next, his eyes came to rest last on Camille, the only one in the crew who seemed to be enjoying the moment. She had her arms tightly around the shoulders of Sam and Raj, like a young athlete with her teammates before the cameras. Instead of Van Zyl, the photo depicted his mother's arm around nothing.

"Hey," Sam said. His voice turned the UN soldier back towards the group. Her silver nameplate glimmered in the sun.

"Yes, Samson?"

Sam's mind reached towards the woman, expecting a metal-on-metal brushback. Instead, what he felt were warm, inviting waves. He quickly jumped out, instinctively realizing that basking very long in that pleasant haze would be agreeing to die.

"Samael," Sam said. Her black eyes gleamed like a quick camera flash. Like an angel's eyes? Or a devil's? In any case, Samael was suddenly the most beautiful person he had ever seen.

"You killed my friends," Sam said.

"Not so," Samael said. "That's not what I do, Samson. You should know better than to suspect me of zealotry. No, I've never been all about martyrdom and sacrifice like some others. But perhaps your passion for matters beyond your ken killed your friends. And yet you made it here for your little court hearing. You, and the Kritalsh girls and my old friend with them. Hello, Van Zyl. Not everyone back home is so interested in your lawsuit, though. But so be it. You ready?"

Samael's eyes moved to Van Zyl, and Camille, then his mother, and finally back to Sam. Sam flashed back to an Enoch passage from his dream.

And I went with the Holy Angels to another place. And there were seven splendid mountains, each different from the other. And three mountains were in the east, and strengthened by being placed one upon the other, and three were towards the south, strengthened in a similar manner. There were likewise deep valleys. And the seventh mountain was in the midst of them. In length they all resembled the seat of a throne.

They were in a field surrounded by mountains, and Samael was not with them anymore. Seven mountains of similar size towered above them and then seemed closer, and closer, yet they shrank as they came until they weren't mountains, but thrones, and the beings on them looked all the same, yet also like different creatures who themselves shifted from one thing to another until they stopped, the seven of them with six equidistant from each other on similar thrones and one at a common wooden table by the side. The one at the small table was Samael, still in her UN fatigues, with the beret resting in front of her beside a thick book. The others were neither men nor women, nor creatures known on Earth, but shifting and reshaping bundles of light on thrones.

Amelia stood just behind Sam to his left, Camille and his mother on either side of Johannes, with Barnabus, who looked so small now, Raj, and Nguyen together behind them.

"Gabriel, God's messenger who presides over paradise," Samael said. She spoke softly, but her words echoed through what was no longer a valley but a chamber with stone walls and floor and large windows opening on all four sides onto endless water.

"Michael, the leader of God's army who commands the nations. Sarakiel, who presides over the spirits of transgressors. Raguel, who presides over justice and who inflicts righteous punishment upon or grants redemption to the world. Raphael, the healer and patron of travelers. Uriel, the eyes of God who presides over hell. Thank you, Holy Ones, for appearing to resolve this dispute."

Each judge became apparent as Samael named them. Gabriel and Michael sat in the middle, with Uriel and Raphael on Sam's right and Raguel and Sarakiel on Sam's left. The Archangels suddenly regarded Sam patiently from what appeared to be settled human forms. Gabriel, a distinguished white man with a gray crew cut, Michael, a young, muscular, white man with long brown hair in a ponytail. Sarakiel, a stern, thin, middle-aged Indian woman with jet-black hair pulled tightly into a bun. Raguel, a young, heavyset Black woman, barely more than a teenager to Sam's eyes. Raphael, an imposing Asian man with glasses and pursed lips. And Uriel, a rather obese, bald Asian man, the only one among them smiling—the sunny disposition of one presiding over clamor and terror. Instead of robes they wore matching black suits.

"I note that the six of you are familiar with this matter," Sam said, "as you are the very same group who condemned and imprisoned my clients for seventy generations under the Earth, a term that has now been served."

He spoke softly, and his words came out as they always did, without the placid resonance of Samael's.

"However, and respectfully," Samael said, standing, "Mr. Young cites no authority for this extraordinary relief—entry into Heaven as if the sin never happened. Not my decision, of course, but redemption seems rather extreme."

"This petition urges the Council to exercise mercy," Sam said. "The suffering undergone has been sufficient. Nearly five thousand years ago, my client and his cohorts broke a well-known rule by coming to Earth and creating offspring with humans. They willingly consented to be tried for that offense, and you, Your Honor Raphael, bound my client and cast him into Hell, where he stayed for seventy generations."

The judges seemed to be listening, not really interested but not quite bored.

"I am here with two requests. One, that my client and the other Angels who committed the sin, having served their punishment of seventy generations under the Earth, and many years on Earth thereafter, return to Heaven. And two, that their offspring, represented here by Trinity and Fifika Kritalsh, be granted their choice about whether to reside on Earth forever or join the race of humans. If these requests are granted, the remaining children of these angels will eventually choose death and judgment, over eternal life on Earth, and that no such children shall be born again once Azazel and the rest of the two hundred return to Heaven."

Samael rose again. "Enoch stood before you and argued on behalf of the very same defendants who form class one of Mr. Young's lawsuit, and this council rightly decided against them. I don't deny that forgiveness, or at least leniency, is sometimes appropriate for a member of the Heavenly Host, particularly when one's penance can be of aid to Heaven and Earth in the future. We all know leniency is proper in some such cases, especially if the accused is willing and able to serve humbly in the future and such service is important enough. But Mr. Young makes no such argument for his clients, as he rightly cannot. He suggests to the Council of God that redemption can be granted from *mercy*. One could argue, though I would beg to differ, that a proposed, though heretofore un-enacted, New Covenant suggests a form of merciful redemption. But such redemption, though discussed years ago, has never been widely granted, and in any case would be only for humans. None of Mr. Young's clients are humans, are they? Just a humble opinion."

Sam saw in Samael's placating demeanor and deference to the panel a crafty power that ran below them and out of their reckoning like a cool stream flowing quietly below a city.

"I have three witnesses to call before I argue the case," Sam said. "May I proceed?"

"You may," Gabriel said. "But I for one agree with our investigator in this respect. Your client, our former brother who stands before us, is not entitled to be judged by the New Covenant, even if such a covenant is held to exist. This is not to say I've formed a judgment about this matter. Or to suggest that you, Mr. Young, are relying on such an argument. But let's be clear. The redemption prayed for by our brother Jesus is for humanity, if indeed anyone at all."

"Thank you, sir."

Very careful not to reach his mind towards the panel, Sam merely glanced slowly from one judge to the next in awaiting follow-up comments. When none came forth, he began.

"I call Johannes Van Zyl."

Van Zyl strode past Sam and stood in front of the panel.

"Could you state your name and tell the court a little bit about yourself, please?" Sam asked.

"We know him," Raguel said. She spoke with the defiant voice of a confident American high schooler sassing the substitute teacher. "Hello again," she said to Van Zyl.

"Yes, quite well, actually," Uriel said, smiling and nodding enthusiastically. "No need for a long introduction." He motioned across his body with a gracious hand, as if making an invitation of sorts. But Sam could see that Uriel's friendly manner belied a power skepticism, much like that of the laughing Buddha, depicted in art carrying his sack of meager possessions down the road to enlightenment. Sam knew judges like this. Sugary sweet in demeanor but unapologetic in their core belief in retribution.

"Seems so long since we spoke," Sarakiel said, "and yet not so long." She sat rigid, elbows on the sides of her throne. In the place of the white dress shirt worn by the others, her tight black turtleneck blended with her suit. Her tightly-pulled-back hair completed the frame around her wizened, olive-skinned face, and her teeth were white like stars in the dark sky.

Van Zyl nodded to her, the first reaction he had made as far as Sam could see from behind. Whether it was an acknowledgment of a closer connection, he could only guess. He made no effort to see the minds of his hosts or of Van Zyl, having been scared quickly out of Samael's pleasant inner life, and ashamed of his arrogance in the attempt.

"Good afternoon," Michael said to Van Zyl. Michael held what looked at first like a cane across his lap but was in fact a short sword, whose sheath was simultaneously every color and no color at all. "Mr. Young, I know your client and his associates from our prior judgment very well, so we can move past all that. We all fought together as soldiers long before I joined in judgment against them. And sir—" He shifted his eyes to Van Zyl. "I can assure you that neither your prior service in Heaven nor our later judgment against you will control our decision here. Welcome, and you will be heard."

Raphael merely nodded to Van Zyl. Gabriel remained impassive, just watching Van Zyl, like a poker player waiting for an opponent's next move.

"Your Honor Michael, if I may," Samael said. "Mr. Young's position before the court is that the prior judgment should be altered such that complete redemption should be extended to his clients. That issue was resolved long ago. Or perhaps not. I am here only to note issues for the court."

Samael, while submissive, even groveling, in words, was majestic in manner, and Sam felt even smaller than when he had been standing behind Van Zyl.

"Good afternoon, my former brothers and sisters," Van Zyl said. His voice was much like the one Sam remembered from the phone, though bolder now, echoing like Samael's and seeming to speak with the combined accent of all the languages on Earth.

"At least, I was once your brother and humbly seek to be so again. My name is now Johannes Van Zyl. I was given that name by my parents when I was born in 1847 in South Africa after seventy generations in the fire below the Earth, where I was sent after you, Your Honor Raphael, righteously bound me for my sins. I am here to beg your forgiveness for me, my fellow sinners, and importantly, for our children, who bear no fault in those ancient transgressions. My real name, given to me by God when I was created in Heaven, is Azazel."

CHAPTER
TWENTY-THREE

"DO YOU ADMIT TO the acts for which you have been previously sentenced?" Sam asked.

"I never made a secret of my acts at the time, and admitted to them when first confronted. I was arrogant and wrongly believed I was entitled to do what I did. I and my fellow transgressors appealed to this Court through Enoch, who walked in human form in Heaven, to plead our case. That appeal was denied, and I served my punishment in fire below the Earth for four thousand nine hundred human years."

"What, in your words, were your acts?" Sam asked.

"Before the creation of the universe or the Earth, God created the Angelic Host, and all the universe and all the Earth were created to be inhabited by the Angels. Or so we hoped."

Azazel extended his hand in front of him, plainly denoting his inclusion of the judges into his claimed belief.

"And, 'in the beginning, God created the Heavens and the Earth,' as the Bible says in its first verse, and 'all of the Sons of God rejoiced in its creation,' as is recorded in Job 38:7. Indeed, Your Honors Sarakiel and Uriel, I remember well that we rejoiced together about the creation that we hoped, even believed, was meant for us."

"Objection," Samael said. "If it please the court, I propose that the witness not directly address the members of the panel. This is merely his testimony. He has not earned the right to a conversation as if with equals."

"He's not asking for a response from the panel," Sam said, surprising himself by speaking at all. Again, his voice felt small following Samael's. "He merely made a statement."

"I agree," Uriel said. He sat on his throne with one leg crossed over the other and both hands folded over his prodigious belly. "And what rules govern this proceeding anyway? Azazel, I also remember what you describe. We were very, very wrong in our hopes, but I do not deny it was as you say."

"Many Angels came to the Earth on the strength of that hope and ruled it as their own," Azazel said. "And neither I nor any of the judges on this panel joined them. As the Bible's second sentence conveys, the 'Earth was formless and void.' But the Bible fails to convey that eons passed between these first two verses, which could more properly read, 'After creation of the Angelic Host, God created the Heavens and the Earth, but the Earth became a state of chaos and waste.'"

"Objection," Samael said. "Irrelevant. This matter turns on whether these transgressors deserve redemption, and not on Azazel's view of history. His answer is, moreover, not responsive to the question, which was about what *he* has done."

"What he has *done* can't be described without context," Sam said. "Any discrepancies in his testimony can be pointed out through cross-examination."

"Overruled," Gabriel said. "We all know the history, so no reason to dwell on it more than necessary to make the point, if there is one."

"God created the Earth," Azazel said, "and we thought it was for us, his only creations. Some, however, actually claimed the Earth for themselves until God, as described in verse three of the Book of Genesis, said 'Let there be light,' thus exposing the transgression, and a conflict ensued in which we all took part."

Though standing behind Azazel, Sam perceived the slightest change in his relaxed but upright posture. He had glanced at Samael.

"Objection," Samael said. "This testimony is well beyond any point." She had remained standing since her last objection, vigilant and beautiful, though, for the first time, her voice betrayed the slightest hint of passion for a cause.

"Overruled," Gabriel said. "But the testimony may now move on to *his* deeds."

"After the angelic conflict," Azazel said, "when Your Honor Michael and your army defeated the rebels, they were shown leniency."

"Objection!" Samael said. "He's referring directly to members of the court again. This is a matter that I mentioned before, and—"

"And the objection was overruled before," Gabriel said.

"The story continues through the creation of humans," Azazel said. "Generations passed and humans multiplied. But as related by Genesis 6:4, some of us came to Earth and, regrettably, mated with human women out of lust—which I knew violated God's law—thus creating offspring never desired by God. I was a member of this group, a leader of this group, and I am truly sorry. I can say only that I never intended to do harm. Unlike the rebels who fought God's army, I and my fellow transgressors, when challenged, declined to fight and subjected ourselves to the authority of this court. Your Honor Michael, I ask you, did you have to gather an army against me? Did I willingly agree to be tried? Did—"

"Objection," Samael said. "He's demanding an answer from the panel now, and the subject matter is outside the scope of the original question."

"He asked a rhetorical question," Sam said. "It needs no answer."

"Sustained," said Gabriel. "Next question."

"Can you describe for the Court the experience of your time in the fire?" Sam asked.

Azazel gazed slowly across the panel and stopped at Samael.

"No. But I would wish it on no one. I am sorry for what I did, and pledge myself to serve God in the Angelic Host if granted redemption. As for our children, they played no role in what we are discussing."

"I have no further questions."

Gabriel turned his head towards Samael, who already stood, hands folded across her chest.

"Azazel, you've testified that you are truly sorry for your transgression?"

"Yes."

"And part of your transgression was, in fact, that you *knew* mating with humans was against God's law before you did it?"

"Yes."

"And unlike the so-called rebels you have referenced, you had no reason to believe your actions were lawful or deserved."

"That's true. But I dispute that they believed their actions were sanctioned."

"And your counsel has stated that your punishment has been sufficient. You heard that, I presume?"

"Yes."

"And you learned something from this punishment, I would imagine."

"Many things."

"When you and your cohorts came to Mount Hermon, you made a vow together against God."

"No."

"Now, that's interesting, Azazel. I have heard no alternate version before. No vow against God? By all common accounts—"

"Objection," Sam said. "The questioner is testifying, not questioning."

"Sustained," Gabriel said. "Let's get to the point and move on."

"No oath, so you say?" Samael said.

"We made an oath. Two hundred of us. But the oath was not against God."

Samael paced across the front of the panel, stopped, and looked down with her hand on her chin, focusing her penetrating gaze on Azazel. It was the same look, the camera-flash look, that she had given Sam at the summit. This time, though, maybe she didn't see it all. Sam knew not to reach towards Samael's mind, but he did not need mind reading to see that Samael struggled over whether to ask an open-ended question. And Azazel's mind would be like metal on metal to her.

"All right, what oath then?"

"Knowing we were committing a transgression by coming to Earth without a mission, and a greater one by engaging with humans without express direction, we vowed to each other that if one of us were punished, we would all be punished together. That none of us in the endeavor would be abandoned by the others. That in our defiance, we would act with loyalty to each other. Not, however, against God as a general matter."

"And who insisted on this oath?'

"I did, and Samyaza."

"You led the conspiracy."

"I've already said the same."

"And this is not an oath against God?"

"No. We were breaking a rule, but we were loyal to God, as we saw it. Almost all of us had fought against—"

"Objection." Samael extended her palm towards Azazel and turned towards the panel. "The witness is being nonresponsive, Your Honors. I humbly suggest we move forward with a new line of questioning."

Not one member of the panel responded.

"And your engagements, as you call them, with humans, produced offspring."

"Some did."

"And the offspring infected the human race with evil. Like demons among the people."

"No. Not so."

"Really? You don't cease to amaze. And whatever happened to these offspring?"

"They were eventually killed."

"And by whom?"

"Some, in a flood. Some, in war. Some were persecuted and slaughtered."

"They were killed by God's order."

"I don't see it that way."

"You are bold, Azazel, but Scripture, the Book of Enoch, is clear on this point. Raphael 'bound Azazel hand and foot, and cast him into darkness, and hurled stones upon him, covering him in darkness,' and then God said to Gabriel, 'Go to the reprobates, to the children of fornication, the offspring of the transgressors, bring them forth, and let them perish by mutual slaughter, for length of days shall not be theirs.'"

"I'm familiar with the passage."

"And yet you say God did not kill them all?"

"Yes."

"Sir, you were imprisoned before God ordered the destruction of the offspring, would you agree?"

"I was imprisoned within one living generation of my transgression."

"That's a yes?"

"Yes."

"My question, sir, is that if you were imprisoned *before* God ordered the destruction of the children of fornication, how did you learn that God did *not* order them all killed?"

"My dispute is not about whether all were killed, but whether they remained dead, and whether the God I knew would specifically order such a cruel slaughter."

"All right." Raphael spoke for the first time. He removed his wire-framed glasses and wiped them, and his eyes, unobstructed, were green and wrinkleless, like a child's. "Unless Gabriel disagrees, I believe we can move on from this question. What's before us is whether Azazel should be granted redemption, and whether any offspring of the transgressors survived or who killed them does not inform the issue."

Gabriel nodded in agreement, and Samael's eyes narrowed.

"But Your Worships, Mr. Young's lawsuit argues for a remedy for two classes, Azazel and his cohorts as well as their offspring. Surely the fact that God has already ordered the destruction of the offspring is relevant to part two. Just my view, by way of suggestion."

"Not so," Sam said. "First, it is not at all clear that God ordered the destruction of all the children of the Angels. In fact, Samael is aware that some live, and the evidence is before you in this very chamber. But even if God issued such an order, this lawsuit seeks to reverse that decision, praying, as it does, that the children of Azazel and the others be free to choose to live as humans."

"Both issues are before the court for a ruling, Samael," Gabriel said, "regardless of prior decisions, but your point is made. Are we almost through with Azazel?"

"Indeed." Samael turned back to the witness. "Even before you transgressed, you were already quite knowledgeable about your role in Heaven, am I right?"

"Of course."

"What is the role of an Archangel in Heaven?

"That's a complicated question. There are so many roles, and they evolve for each of us."

"Simplify it, then."

"How simple would you like it? How would you crystallize the role you've played, Samael?"

Samael faced the court. "Pardon me, Your Worships, but I ask that the witness not address me by name or ask me questions. As I have argued to you, this is not a conversation. He is being examined at a trial in which *he* is the subject. He should merely answer the questions. Just my view, of course, but it is my duty to bring such matters to your attention."

"There are no set rules for this proceeding," Uriel said, holding his arms out to his side. Legs still crossed, Uriel bounced his foot rhythmically as if he were quietly enjoying some music.

"Just an idea, Your Honor," Samael said. "Perhaps for efficiency, we could move forward with only yes or no questions."

"I'm likin' Azazel's answers so far," Raguel said. "I mean, there are roles, and they do evolve. And as my role has been specifically to judge those in transgression of God's laws, I will speak on this, if it's no bother to Gabriel." Raguel slouched on her throne now, legs extended in front of her. Not only to suggest boredom, Sam surmised, but equally to settle in for what could be a long lecture. She crossed her knee-length, high-heeled black boots like a confident high school cutup.

Gabriel nodded, still impassive.

"I'd like to hear our investigator's answer to the witness's question," Raguel said. The panel watched Samael closely, and she nodded again, almost as if to bow.

"The role of God's servant in Heaven is to rule Heaven and Earth," Samael said, "under God's name, of course." She looked to Azazel.

"I would say the role is instead to abide in Heaven and *tend* to the Earth," Azazel said.

"It was your special brand of tending that caused so much trouble, was it not?"

"A fair point, Samael, but as far as you ruling *under God's name*, I think we—"

"Objection!" Samael said. "Azazel is attempting to debate me about long-resolved matters that are not before this court. I suggest we move on."

"Then do so," Gabriel said. He had been, all along, watching Samael and, in turn, Azazel, through hooded, half-shut eyes, resting his head on his throne. "And please just answer the questions, Azazel."

"After your punishment was served, you were born in South Africa in 1847."

"Yes."

"And you have lived on Earth since then, in human form it seems."

"Yes."

"And you met Cinderella Baptista in Buenos Aires, Argentina, in 1937, when Trinity/Camille was born."

"Yes."

"You encountered her daughter, Fifika Kritalsh, in 1958 aboard a boat leaving Buenos Aires."

"Yes."

"You met Fifika Kritalsh again in 1982, when she was Marcela Young, in Washington, DC."

"Yes."

"And you met her sister, Trinity Kritalsh, later known as Alifair Roja, and now known as Camille Paradisi, in 2014 in Virginia."

"Yes."

Samael turned her back to Azazel for a moment, hand on her chin as if in thought. She turned back around. "You're the father of Fifika Kritalsh, also known as Marcela Young, and Trinity Kritalsh, also known as Camille Paradisi?"

"Yes."

"When did it come to your attention that you would be the lead claimant in this lawsuit? The one claiming that you're ever so sorry for your lust, that you have redeemed yourself, and that you've been punished enough?"

Azazel paused for a moment. He leaned back a bit and seemed to regard the panel.

"I'd say about five years ago."

Samael faced the panel now, nodding quietly to herself, and then her eyes darted to Sam's and rested there.

"What is the name of your youngest child?"

"Alifair Andrada," Azazel said.

"And you spawned her only four years ago, after you planned to summon this council."

"Yes."

"And who is her mother?"

"Camille Paradisi."

"Your own daughter."

"Yes."

"And you also had relations with Fifika Kritalsh, otherwise known as Marcela Young back in 1981."

"However you want to put it . . . yes," Azazel said.

"She's your own daughter."

"Yes."

"And what result did that unseemly coupling produce?"

Azazel placed both hands on his lower back as if to stretch, and breathed deeply one time as the panel—all but Gabriel, it seemed—listened intently.

"Objection," Sam said, a little late. He said it instinctively, as the question contained an argumentative fact that rendered it impossible to answer without agreeing to the offending portion. But his heart lifted just a bit as he saw the slightest hint of a smile cross Gabriel's face.

"Sustained," Gabriel said.

"Who is your child with Marcela Young?" Samael asked.

"Samson Young."

"Your attorney."

"Yes."

"Archangel of tending, indeed." She walked, arms folded, closer to Azazel. "Mr. Van Zyl, have you ever heard of the word, what is it, *preservatif*? Condom? A rubber?"

"Objection," Sam said. "Argumentative."

"Oh, indeed!" Samael said. "But this is an argument, one I thought was long over and decided, but I suppose Azazel feels the need to drag this court into session to point out that his cause, a lost one back when Enoch argued it, has become even weaker. Good to know, but I wonder about the point of it all. Perhaps another seventy generations are in order to see if Azazel can learn to keep his trousers zipped."

"Objection sustained," Gabriel said. "You've brought no new charges against Azazel, though you likely knew all of this long before now."

"I have not," Samael said. "It's all rather sad, though. Azazel dragging his raggedy group of bastards here—for what? To grovel at us like we're municipal constables? I have nothing further." Samael turned her back to Azazel and glanced at Sam as she returned to her seat.

"Azazel," Sam said. "Have you consorted with a human since your release?"

"No."

"And to your understanding, does God's law prohibit relations between an Angel on Earth and a hybrid?"

"To my knowledge, the question has never been addressed. I think the Council may, until now, have held the belief that our offspring had all been destroyed."

"To your knowledge, have any other Heavenly... personages, I guess I would say, had relations with hybrids on Earth?"

"Objection," Samael said. "Azazel and his children are the subject of this hearing, and only them."

"The court's investigator has leveled an accusation," Sam said. "Her personal standards in this regard are relevant."

"My leniency in declining to convene this court to punish Azazel for his recent dalliances may be instructive," Samael said. "But opening this hearing to cover all similar conduct by the Heavenly Host would be most unwise, Your Honor Gabriel. Very unwise."

Gabriel and Michael exchanged glances.

"Objection sustained."

CHAPTER
TWENTY-FOUR

GABRIEL NODDED TO AZAZEL, who turned and strode past Sam. His eyes blazed, but with what? Sam had to stop himself from reaching towards Azazel's mind.

"Who's your next witness?" Gabriel asked.

"I call Cinderella Baptista," Sam said.

Samael stood and surveyed the chamber. "Is that witness present?"

"She's not," Sam said. "I can't have been expected to know every issue that would arise in this trial, but it appears to me that given Samael's line of inquiry regarding Azazel's intimate relations, I need Cinderella Baptista as a witness."

"But you don't have her," Samael said. "Your Honors, I humbly suggest to you that Mr. Young is playing games. He well knew the issues before the Court and should have prepared accordingly."

"Nevertheless," Sam said, "it's hard to imagine that this esteemed court would rule on a matter of this significance without hearing all the evidence. If the fault for not producing this witness falls to me, so be it. That doesn't change the problem."

"Your Worships, I agree that we need to get past this petty matter so the members of the court can attend to what I am sure is pressing business beyond my understanding, but allowing Mr. Young to simply *state* facts deprives me of the ability to cross-examine the source of the information. It would be quite irregular."

"This witness is important," Sam said. "There's a critical element to our petition that only her testimony can provide."

"Is there anyone else who can testify on her behalf?" Raguel asked. "Or tell us what she would have said?"

"Objection," Samael said. "Mr. Young should be prepared. Such testimony would be hearsay."

Sam faced the panel, making eye contact with each member.

"It's not ideal," he said. "But I call Rajniriput Buterab."

"A human?" Samael said. "We're taking testimony from humans now?"

"I was aware of no rule to the contrary," Sam said, "and would point out that humans have shared information with Heaven, both directly and indirectly, always. Adam, Enoch, Noah, Abraham, Jacob, Moses, Joshua, Elijah—"

"Overruled," Gabriel said. "Enoch litigated before this very court."

"In this very same matter, I might add," Samael said. "And lost rather badly, as I recall."

Raj passed Sam and stood before the panel.

"State your name for the court, please," Sam said.

"Raj Buterab."

"Tell the panel a bit about yourself."

"I was born in Plovdiv, Bulgaria, in 1939. I lived there until I was seventeen years old, when my father brought me to America. I grew up in Bennet County, Virginia."

"What do you do for living?"

"My father had an import-export business, and I pretty much did that, too. Lately I've been running a charity. Raising money for Roma people in Eastern Europe."

"Are you Roma?"

"I am."

"Do you know Cinderella Baptista?"

"I do."

"How do you know her?"

"I met her in Sofia, Bulgaria, in 1989, right around the time the Soviet Union collapsed. I was there on business, and I met her at a restaurant. I was there for a meeting, and she was serving drinks. We're both Roma, and she recognized that right away, and I hung around after the meeting and we became friends."

"Tell us more about that."

"We had a relationship for about ten years. I was back and forth between the US and Eastern Europe a lot back then. For my business, importing cars to Turkey, China, and Eastern Europe. And she helped me there, too. She could make people believe anything. I mean, it was like she could read minds and push people, even government officials, even police, to make decisions she urged. Which was big for my business."

"Why?"

Sam could not see Raj's face, but he knew exactly what expression it carried just then. The wry smirk.

"Some people thought my business wasn't properly attentive to regulations and that sort of thing."

"Did you come to learn anything unusual about her?" Sam asked.

"Lots of things. I always knew she had mental-health difficulties. She was manic depressive or something, or so I thought. You know the type. But it was different than that, too. Finally, after many years of acquaintance, we were together in

Sofia at her apartment. It was more like a hotel, a really nice new place I paid for through the business. And she was very drunk. She told me she had been born in 1825, that she was immortal, that she had died several times before and always came back as if nothing had happened. She had even killed herself before. We were arguing because I wanted to get her some help, some real treatment, at a hospital in America. We were standing on the balcony at her apartment, which was on the fifteenth floor downtown. She was acting crazy, yelling, wanting me to believe her, which, of course, I didn't. And then she jumped."

"She jumped from the fifteenth floor?"

"Yeah. I ran downstairs. At that point there was no point calling the cops just yet. No one could have survived that fall onto concrete. It was past midnight and no one was around. So, I'm thinking, I don't know what I'm gonna do. By the time I got there, she was just sitting on the steps, covered in blood but alive."

"What happened next?"

"We talked all night. She wasn't drunk anymore, and she started proving to me what she was. She could make stuff fly around the apartment, telekinesis or whatever. She knew things about me I'd never told her. She told me about her children. She had lots of children, going way back, but the only ones still living were two daughters and a son, and she had died giving birth to the son. She hadn't seen them in years. She said one of her daughters and her son, who was a priest, lived in Northern Virginia, which is where I lived. She said her daughters were like her but that the son, the priest, and her other children weren't. She said she was going crazy and there was no stopping it. That she had lived too long and her brain was slowly frying, like an egg in a pan. That's how she put it."

"What did you do?" Sam said.

"I brought Cinderella to the US and got her checked into a psychiatric hospital. And then I set out to fulfill my promise to her."

"Which was what?"

"To find her kids, to help them."

"What did that mean, to help them?"

"At first it meant financially. That's all I knew, all I thought I *could* do. But when I met them, it kind of changed."

"Who are Cinderella's children?"

"Paul Andrada, rest in peace, and Marcela Young and Camille Paradisi. They're right over there."

"Did you help them?"

"Sure, Marcela and I were part of a group of friends. She studied religion, and I eventually met Camille, too. And Paul, I paid for his house up at Holy Angels, helped out with all kinds of stuff up there. And with Marcela's son, too."

"Who is Marcela's son?"

"You."

"You said something about things changing once you met them."

"Yeah," Raj said. "I came to believe in it. That they weren't fully human. We started our project."

"What project?"

"To get the curse lifted."

"The curse?"

"Whatever you want to call it. The destiny of Cinderella and those like her to never be able to die. To become insane as they aged with no hope for relief."

"How did you go about trying to lift the curse?"

"Good question. Mostly, for them, it was studying. Marcela studied religion, and Camille was a nun. They had started along that path before they met me. But in part, it became about seeing if we could locate more people like them. And then Camille had an idea."

"What was it?"

"That they should seek a trial. Like in the old days in the

Bible, when people would reach out directly to God. She also had the idea that you, Sam, should be the person to do it."

"I have a few questions, Mr. Buterab," Uriel said, his usual Buddha-like placidity replaced by a stern scowl. "So, they *all* want to be humans? They all want to die?"

"Someday, they will."

"And you suggest that we change their nature?" Uriel asked. "Meddle with God's creations? Change them biologically?"

"Objection," Sam said. "Mr. Buterab is only a fact witness, not a lawyer or a party to the case. Neither is he an expert on religion, nor has he been offered as such. But I will answer your question. It's plain you can achieve the result we ask for if you wish to do so, whether that requires a biological change or not. And if a biological change is the stumbling block, what about evolution on Earth? All of God's creatures have evolved biologically."

"Evolved naturally on Earth, through processes put in place by God. Not by a magic trick emanating from this council, Mr. Young."

Uriel leaned back in his seat, hands on his stomach, smiling again. But his eyes, still on Sam's, narrowed.

"Mr. Buterab," Sarakiel said, "you mentioned persons on Earth reaching out to God, 'in the old days in the Bible,' to use your words. Could you elaborate?"

"Sure. It seems to me that Heaven used to be more involved."

"Is that a criticism, Mr. Buterab?" Sarakiel said. "And how would you know what level of involvement Heaven has had on Earth, and when?"

Raj took a deep breath. "Maybe it is. And I don't."

"Thank you," Sarakiel said.

"I have a few more questions, Mr. Buterab," Sam said. "Why isn't Cinderella Baptista with us here today?"

Raj paused, as if to give form to his thoughts. "Cinderella is in a mental hospital in Havana. She's a stark raving lunatic, I'm sorry to say. She rarely communicates in any intelligible way. Mostly cries, screams, and curses all day. They give her medication, which does nothing except provide occasional sleep. It's like her body is her own personal—and apparently eternal—Hell."

"That's all I have," Sam said.

"I have a few questions for Mr. Buterab," Samael said. She stood and approached Raj, arms clasped behind her back. "Sir, it seems you've studied a bit of religion."

"A small bit, compared to many."

"And you heard the testimony of Azazel just now, right?"

"Yes."

"It seems that Baptista and the Kritalsh sisters, if Azazel speaks the truth, were fathered by an Angel and are thus without a biological human father."

"It could be so. I thought the court was deciding that, and if so, what should be done about it."

"Can you think of anyone from religious history, Mr. Buterab, who was similarly spawned by a deity?"

"Strike the question," Gabriel said. "Move on." Gabriel glared hard at Samael as she took her seat.

"I have one more question," Sam said. "Did Cinderella Baptista ever tell you why she thinks she's the way she is?"

"Yes, she told me the night she jumped, way back when," Raj said. "She said her father was the Devil."

CHAPTER
TWENTY-FIVE

"NEXT WITNESS," GABRIEL SAID.

"My next witness is Nguyen Jones."

Nguyen passed on Sam's right, and Sam expected to feel his mind on fire, but instead he noticed barely more angst than normal. Interesting.

"State your name for the court," Sam said.

"Objection," Samael said. "Another human."

"Overruled," Gabriel said. "You may answer."

"Nguyen Jones."

"What do you do for a living?"

"I'm an investigator for the law firm of Young and Griffin in Bennet County, Virginia, USA," Nguyen said. "Earth."

"Were you the investigator for the case of Commonwealth of Virginia versus Camille Paradisi in 2015?"

"Yes."

"What about the case of Commonwealth of Virginia versus Igor Alexi in 2019?"

"Yes."

"Are you familiar with the case files—our files, the court files, and the Virginia Department of Forensic Science files—for those two cases?"

"Very familiar."

"Can you tell the court about the DNA evidence in the Paradisi case?"

"Camille Paradisi was charged with the murder of a guy named Zebulon Lucas. DNA evidence was found on his hat, and that DNA matched the DNA profile of Ms. Paradisi."

"Was there anything unusual about that DNA profile?"

"Yes. According to—"

'Objection," Samael said. "This man is not a scientist. He's not competent to give testimony on this question."

"Frankly," Sam said, "that's technically accurate, but he is familiar with the reports in the case and has spoken personally with the scientists involved. More importantly, though, I did not believe the court would wish to parade through the half dozen witnesses necessary to make this point under the normal rules of evidence."

"Keep movin'," Raguel said with a wave of her hand. Sam noted for the first time her bright-red nail polish. She glanced at her nails.

"Camille Paradisi's DNA contains only one set of genetic markers instead of two, as with humans. Each human receives one set of genes from each parent. She has only one set."

"What does that mean?"

"I have no idea. Scientists say that the chances of her genes appearing this way, meaning that she received the same genetic marker at all genetic locations from each of her parents, are one in billions, maybe trillions. Some have opined that it means she's not human. Others have said Paradisi's genes look that way by random coincidence."

"What happened in the Paradisi case?"

"Ms. Paradisi was shot and killed before the case went to trial."

"Did you witness this?"

"Yes."

"What did you see?"

"I saw a man fire an automatic rifle at her from close range, and I saw her head come apart. I saw you trying to hold it together. It's been on TV."

"Is she alive now?"

"She's right over there." Nguyen pointed past Sam.

"Can you tell the court about the DNA evidence in the Igor Alexi case?"

"Sure. Igor Alexi is charged with killing his wife. At the crime scene, there was DNA on a light switch matching Mr. Alexi's."

"Anything unusual about that profile?"

"Yeah. As with Paradisi, Mr. Alexi has only one genetic marker at each location."

"What happened with that case?"

"Mr. Alexi pled guilty a few days ago and is asking to receive the death penalty. He's claiming he's died several times before and can't be killed."

"What will happen if he receives the death penalty?"

"Somewhere between six months and a year from now, he'll be executed at a prison in southern Virginia."

"Has the press reported on this, on the claim that he can't be killed?"

"Yes."

"Has the press linked this to the Paradisi case?"

"Yes, especially—"

"Objection," Samael said, approaching the panel. She spoke

barely above a whisper. "You see what he's doing, Your Honors? He's threatening you. Threatening even Him! Change the hybrids to humans or the world will know! The nerve. I strongly urge you not to condone the tactic."

"I'm not sure I understand the objection," Sam said. "I'm merely pointing out that the hybrids die and rise again, one of the many nonhuman things about them, and I'm using the most direct evidence at my disposal to prove it. Resurrections are not that uncommon in human lore and religion. Most notably Jesus, who also lacked a human father, as we know."

"Your Honor Gabriel," Samael said, "now he's mocking *you*. Taunting you. He seeks to compare you to the lustful Azazel. I humbly suggest you do not take it lightly."

Gabriel turned towards Sam.

Sam looked at the stone beneath his feet. "Your Honor Gabriel, I am absolutely not mocking you and never would. I don't even understand Samael's point, with all due respect."

"He understands my point," Samael said. "He understands it well."

"Why don't you educate us, Samael?" Raguel said. "How does this line of questioning mock Gabriel?"

"Luke 1:26 though 27, Your Honors. 'And in the sixth month the angel Gabriel was sent from God unto a city of Galilee, named Nazareth, to a virgin espoused to a man whose name was Joseph, of the house of David; and the virgin's name was Mary.'"

Uriel held his arms out and shrugged.

Samael picked up the book from her small wooden table and flipped through it. She then took a step towards the panel. "Luke 1:28. 'And the Angel Gabriel came *in* unto her.' Mr. Young is approaching an unseemly point, one we've resolved long ago, the matter of Gabriel's visit to Jesus' mother."

The large room sat in silence for a long moment. Sam noted the view through the large windows. The room had been surrounded by pristine blue water an hour ago, but the windows now opened on snowcapped mountains all around. Sam glanced quickly at the panel and saw Gabriel watching him closely.

Gabriel belted out a deep, hearty laugh like one might expect from an Angel. "Objection overruled. I don't think the point Mr. Young is making is the one you suggest, Samael. Although *you* have always been very fond of it. This is the second time you've touched on it today."

Samael set the book down, turned away, and then took her seat.

"You can answer," Sam said to Nguyen.

"The press has made the connection between Paradisi and Alexi. I guess only kind of 'out there' journalists buy into it. But that could change if the Commonwealth of Virginia can't kill Mr. Alexi."

Samael began to stand, but Gabriel's extended hand placed her back in her seat.

"It sure could," Michael said.

"Are you also familiar with the DNA profiles of persons named Riker Lugnudsky, Tawana Hightower, and Esau Jacobs?"

"Yes. Those profiles contain the same anomaly as Paradisi's and Alexi's."

"Have you reviewed a two-page draft report prepared by doctors Juliana Kim and William Pitts about all of the profiles we've discussed?"

"Yes."

"What's its rough conclusion?"

"That assuming these profiles can be confirmed as authentic, the subjects could be a previously undiscovered species."

"Is there anything in that report about these hybrids rising from the dead?"

"No."

"To your knowledge, why not?"

"That fact has not been scientifically established."

"Do Lugnudsky, Hightower, and Jacobs claim to have died

and risen again?"

"Hightower and Jacobs, yes. Lugnudsky, no. But he's kinda young. Born in 1989."

"How old is Camille Paradisi?"

"According to her, eighty-one."

"And her sister?"

"Seventy-seven."

"Hightower?"

"Seventy-three."

"Jacobs?"

"One hundred seventy."

"If Alexi's execution fails to kill him, would that scientifically establish the fact of coming back from the dead?"

"Executions are thoroughly recorded, witnessed, and documented. So, yes, especially if they try and try again."

"That's all the questions I have for this witness," Sam said.

"No questions," Samael said. She leaned back in her small wooden chair, arms folded.

"I've got a question for you, Samael," Uriel said. He leaned forward, towards Samael, his large belly pressing up against his armrest as he leaned onto it with both elbows. For the first time, Sam noticed that he wore sandals with his suit. "I've always believed that the offspring of Azazel, Samyaza, and the other transgressors were killed."

"Yes, Your Honor Uriel. We believed most were killed at the time of the Great Flood. The remainder were killed in wars, most of them by the Israelites in the struggle for the land of Canaan. The Council of God was quite well aware of that war. In fact, we were, at times, involved."

"I remember," Uriel said. "But Mr. Young is saying that these offspring can rise from the dead. Do you dispute that?"

Samael breathed deeply, eyes down at her table, and then raised her head to Uriel.

"I don't know."

"I don't either. So, what I'm wondering about is, if the children of the transgressors can rise from the dead, especially if they always rise from the dead, where are they?"

Samael stood. "All I can think of, sir, is that there were only two hundred transgressors. Maybe all of them didn't have children, and maybe the ones that did only had one, or maybe only a few. So, I suppose, hypothetically, the offspring could still be living on Earth. Maybe there's just not that many of them, especially compared to today's population. I assure you it's not a problem of magnitude."

"Maybe there's not that many of them," Raphael said. "But what about their offspring?"

Samael sat. "To my knowledge, sir, if they exist they don't often produce hybrid offspring. Unless perhaps they breed with each other, which is probably rather rare. It's not as if they're gathered in tribes anymore."

"It sounds as if you know a good bit about these hybrids, Samael," Michael said.

"May I say something?" Sam asked.

"Please."

"While the hybrids may not hand down a manifesting Angel gene when they mate with a human, they certainly can hand down the gene to offspring when mating with another hybrid. More importantly—"

"But they're obviously scattered, likely merely hundreds on a planet with seven billion," Uriel said. "Since when has the Council micromanaged Earth at that level?"

"As I was saying," Sam said, "more importantly, since the release of Azazel and the Fallen Angels, things have changed. Any offspring of Azazel and that group is a hybrid, just like my clients, and are destined for the same fate as Cinderella Baptista. Samael surely knows this, yet advocates for the continuation of the present state of affairs."

"Interesting, very fascinating," Samael said. "He blames his own client for the mess. Hard to disagree with Mr. Young on this point. But the fact remains. This matter does not present a crisis worthy of this panel."

"I've also got some questions for you, Samael," Sarakiel said. "You're still a member of God's Court because, as we all conceded back then, you're pretty good at managing things on Earth, at least in your own way, no?"

"Yes, Your Honor."

"Part of your job is to report back to us so we, and most importantly, God, can separate the wheat from the chaff and make a decision here and there, right?"

"To consult with you about Earthly matters," Samael said. "Of course."

"Okay. So, my question is, why don't we know about any of this?"

Samael, radiant and smiling, stood and approached, coming within several yards of Sarakiel and bowing her head slightly. "It's just not something important enough to warrant the attention of the Council of God."

"Your Honors," Sam said. "Sarakiel's question goes to the heart of the matter. Samael's failure to bring important matters to your attention. Or is she the final arbiter of what's important? The only arbiter?"

"More like the very reverse," Sarakiel said. She leaned forward. Her eyes thoughtfully probed Sam, then rested on Samael. "Is that your view, Samael? That you are the only arbiter? That this kind of issue should not be brought to our attention? Perhaps it's been a while since we examined your standards."

Samael's eyes flashed at Sam before she turned to the panel. "Gabriel, Michael, Sarakiel, Raphael, Raguel, Uriel. With all respect, perhaps it's been a while since you cared."

CHAPTER TWENTY-SIX

"DO YOU HAVE ANY further witnesses, Mr. Young?"

"None."

"Samael?"

Samael stood. "I have one witness, Your Honors."

"Proceed."

"I call Bernard Genoa."

Sam heard soft footsteps behind him and turned. Bernie approached the front of the stone chamber in his standard uniform, though his hair looked like it had been recently combed. He stood in front of the panel and set his briefcase down by his side.

"State your name for the Court, sir."

"Bernard Genoa."

"What do you for a living?"

"I have my own law firm in Bennet County, Virginia. Mostly I do court appointed guardian *ad litem* cases."

"What on Earth is that?" Samael said.

"I am appointed by judges to investigate family-law matters and to make a recommendation to the judge about what is in the best interest of my ward . . . that's like a client."

"In doing such work, do you investigate people's backgrounds?"

"Yes. I collect records, do interviews, and write reports to courts."

"At my request, did you prepare such a report on attorney Samson Young?"

"Yes."

"Do you have it with you today?"

"Yes." Bernie reached into his briefcase and pulled out a manila folder, handing it to Samael. He then turned and provided a similar folder to Sam.

"Your Honors, I move for admission of Heaven's exhibit one."

"Objection," Sam said. "I was given no notice about this report until just now. It could take days to review it and prepare to question this witness. The information is also irrelevant. I'm the lawyer on this case. Not a party. Information about my background adds nothing to your decision."

Gabriel looked towards Samael.

Samael's slitted eyes regarded Sam. "Very, very interesting. I understand Mr. Young to say that he is not part of class two to the lawsuit, that he seeks a remedy for all of the hybrids on Earth, the Canaanites of old, the Nephilim, the Giants of the ancient Holy Land, and the unfortunate, more recent, offspring of Azazel and the other transgressors. But yet, he seeks no remedy at all for himself?"

"Your Honors, there is nothing in those investigative files you don't already know about me."

"Not so," Samael said. "If this trial has proven anything, it's that such details are not common knowledge, and that the Council, with all its other duties, cannot be expected to know about mundane Earthly matters such as Mr. Young's sins, great though they are."

"Mr. Young," Raguel said. "Let's clear this here issue up. Are you a member of class two of the lawsuit?"

Sam could feel his mother and Camille behind him, reaching towards him.

"Yes."

"All right, Samael," Raguel said. "Unless Gabriel objects, I'd say just give us the highlights."

Gabriel nodded.

"Of course," Samael said. "Time better spent than asking the panel to review lengthy materials. I'll take care of that for you, with pleasure, as always."

"Go ahead," Gabriel said.

"By way of proffer, I'd first say that the hybrids of ancient times, the first generation spawned by Azazel's sin, if they are indeed still alive, have likely suffered. And some of those in the more recent generation, spawned by Azazel and others after those transgressors were punished, such as Camille Paradisi and Fifika Kritalsh, have endured difficulties as well. Raised in extreme poverty. Sexually abused by a demented man who shared them with his friends. Eventually abandoned by an insane mother and left to fend for themselves."

Samael regarded Camille and Fifika for a moment then turned to Sam. "But Mr. Young is himself a different story . . . very different. He was raised in a loving family and surrounded by caring mentors, such as Mr. Buterab, and his mother's friends paid his tuition to prestigious schools. And here is my point: unlike his aunt and mother, who sinned while they were young because they knew no better but later devoted their lives to God, Mr. Young has done nothing but use his gifts for personal gain. This report, scrupulously prepared by Mr. Genoa, notes the excellent, indeed, impossible results Mr. Young has achieved in his legal cases. And not to help people, not usually, no, far from it. But for criminals who pay him for service and often continue to prey on society. Mr. Young has been cheating, Your Honors, and doing so for his entire life, and mostly to enrich himself."

Samael flipped through the report and set it down on her table. "And Mr. Young is arrogant, Your Honors. There are many examples, but I submit that the way Mr. Young treats people he believes to be inferior to him is highly instructive. What did Jesus say? 'For whoever is least among you—this one is great.' Mr. Young begs to differ. Bernard Genoa is a man who devotes his life to helping children, which he does with humility and for meager pay. And how does Mr. Young refer to Mr. Genoa? He calls him a bottom feeder. What else did Jesus say of such matters? 'Whoever humbles himself is the greatest in the kingdom of heaven'? And what does Mr. Young ask of you? To allow him to live on Earth in his present state until he decides he wants to become a human. Speaking of Jesus, just think of it, your Honors: Jesus the humble carpenter who used his heavenly gifts to win hearts and save souls, but Mr. Young uses his albeit far lesser skills to enrich himself by whoring for criminals. 'Blessed are the meek,' Jesus said, and it—"

"Enough," Gabriel said. "Jesus and his gifts, from wherever they came, are not relevant to these proceedings nor normally of interest to you, Samael."

"Understood, Your Honor Gabriel. But you see, this is the difficulty with litigating matters in a class action like this. Not all the members of the class are similarly situated, and—"

"Jesus is not a member of this class action! I am ordering you to cease the analogies and references to Jesus."

"I did not suggest that he should be, your Honor Gabriel. In any event, I'll conclude my point. Samson Young does not deserve this Court's mercy, perhaps not even so much as Azazel or the other class members who have at least sacrificed and suffered."

Samael walked across the front of the panel and then turned to face the court. She suddenly smiled, eyes alight, as if an unexpected but pleasant thought had had just occurred to her.

"Your Honor Sarakiel referenced Jesus' Parable of the Weeds. 'The harvester will gather his wheat into the barn and burn up the chaff with unquenchable fire.' But it's so hard, sometimes, to separate the wheat from the chaff, isn't it? Jesus also said, 'Greater love cannot be found than that someone lay down his life for his friends.' Maybe Mr. Young can help his friends. Perhaps this court will be disposed to rule for his friends if he personally serves seventy generations in the fire? Just a humble suggestion."

Samael turned to Sam, her eyes blazing quickly again, like a camera flash.

"Excuse me." Amelia was now beside Sam, facing the panel. "If Samael is finished with this witness, I have a few questions for him."

Gabriel regarded her for a moment and then looked to his right, to Raguel.

"Proceed," Raguel said.

"Mr. Genoa, you prepared this report about Mr. Young at Samael's request?"

"I prepared it at the request of a client who contacted me by phone. I did not know exactly who the client was at the time. Or even now."

"The instructions were conveyed verbally."

"Yes."

"How much have you been paid in this matter?"

Bernie glanced at Samael. "I think that's privileged. Attorney-client privilege."

"It's not at all privileged," Amelia said. "Mr. Genoa may be an attorney, but in this case he's testifying as an investigator. Much like a retained scientist or psychologist, his compensation is always fair game. The widest latitude in cross-examination is, and should be, when counsel explores the critical question of bias."

"Overruled," Gabriel said.

Bernie looked down at his feet. "I was paid two thousand five hundred dollars an hour for my work on this matter, which included some research and some meetings with Mr. Young. But for the report on Mr. Young, I received a separate, flat fee."

Amelia remained quiet until Bernie looked up from the floor and directly at her.

"And?"

"I was paid five hundred thousand dollars for the report."

"Did you speak with Mr. Young about the contents of the report?"

"No."

"Did you interview Nguyen Jones?"

"No."

"Or me?"

"No." Bernie was watching his feet again.

"Judges in Bennet County?"

"No.

"Police officers?"

"No."

"Prosecutors?"

"No."

"How many *pro bono* cases has Mr. Young handled so far in 2019?"

"I have no idea."

"Please tell us how many current or former clients of Mr. Young you interviewed."

"None."

"Bernie, you heard that Mr. Young referred to you as a bottom feeder, right?"

"Yes."

"That hurt your feelings."

"Maybe."

"Did anything about your work on this case involve helping children?"

"No."

"Did anyone else hear Samael provide you the instructions regarding what this report was supposed to be about?"

"No."

"Judges, that's all I have," Amelia said.

"May I say something?" Bernie said. Gabriel regarded Bernie for moment, then turned to Samael.

"Proceed, Mr. Genoa," Samael said.

"It's just that I was never asked to do any of those things. I have a lot of cases, and it's not my normal practice to interview absolutely everyone, to investigate absolutely everything. It's more like I get a feeling about a case, based on, you know, my experience. My training. Then I prepare a report for judges with my input. That's what a guardian *ad litem* does. I'm not used to being questioned and all of this. I just thought you should know that."

"I have one more question for Mr. Genoa," Amelia said. Gabriel nodded. "What exactly is your definition of a bottom feeder?"

CHAPTER
TWENTY-SEVEN

"ARE THERE ANY FURTHER witnesses in this matter?" Gabriel asked.

"Yes," Sam said. "I call Samael."

"Objection!" Samael stood straight, the thick book she held in one hand pressed against her chest. "I'm the Council's investigator. Any past matters concerning me are not relevant to the issues before the court, which are only about Azazel, the other transgressors, and their offspring."

"Samael is an investigator with knowledge of facts highly relevant to the case," Sam said.

Gabriel glanced one way and then another across the panel. "Like what?"

"She's the only . . . personage, I suppose, available to me as a live witness about the actual facts of the crime the class one claimants committed."

"Azazel already admitted his guilt at the time, and he's done so again today," Gabriel said. "You've already questioned him."

"Of course," Sam said. "He's never denied his mistake, but he is not a witness to the full facts of the adjudication that previously occurred, and in all fairness, he's subject to the critique of being biased in his own favor. Besides, only Samael can testify about the disparate treatment handed down by this court in similar matters and what is requested here."

Uriel glared down at him. "Excuse me?"

"Your Honor, Uriel, I meant no offense, only that the panel would obviously want to consider evidence that is universally considered relevant concerning transgressions. In my world, we refer to this sentencing factor as the requirement that a court, in imposing sentencing on an individual, avoid unwarranted disparities between similarly situated defendants. At least that's a rule for courts of the United States. Indeed, the US Supreme Court has held that failure to consider the sentencing factor along with the rest constitutes a basis for reversal of a court's sentence. The case citation is, among others, United States v. Booker, 543 U.S. 220 (2005)."

"We already know about every matter we've ever considered," Raguel said.

"And I can't imagine you'd suggest that a decision from a court on Earth binds this panel," Uriel said.

"I'm quite sure you all remember your prior adjudications against members of Heaven," Sam said, "even over the eons during which you've each sat on this honorable court. But it's my job to place such history into context to help avoid unreasonable disparities. And the precedent I cited is certainly not binding, merely capable of being considered persuasive, if it becomes so in your wise view."

"He's straying outside the bounds of propriety," Samael said. "The deeds of others from the past, of any other member of the Heavenly Host, are irrelevant. We are here concerning Azazel."

"May I point out that Samael just called a witness for no other purpose than to attack my character. I voiced no objection, though the testimony was worthless to her cause. Only Your Honors can decide where to place the weight of your wisdom, not I, and not Samael either. She's not a member of this panel, merely the Council's investigator, and in this matter she and I stand on equal footing."

Gabriel and Michael exchanged looks.

"Let's complete the hearing," Gabriel said. "You may question Samael on relevant, and only truly relevant, matters."

"I have one more request," Sam said. "As Samael is now taking part in this hearing as herself, and not as the Council's investigator, I submit to the Court that she should appear before the Court in her true personage."

"Objection!" Samael said. "Who does Mr. Young, a hybrid of all things, think he is? Next, he'll challenge the members of the court to appear to his eyes as he wishes. The panel is losing control of this hearing."

"We have lost control of nothing!" Michael's voice boomed off the walls of the chamber. He stood on his throne, sheathed sword now in his hand. "By what notion do you suggest that any ruling concerning you would apply to an Archangel? You are the Council's investigator and will abide by the rulings of the panel and stay in order."

Samael bowed slightly.

"Call the witness," Gabriel said.

"I call Samael," Sam said.

Samael, still in UN fatigues, transformed into a thin, middle-aged white man with jet-black hair and wizened features. He had the face of one who was inclined to be severe, perhaps even brash or angry, but who had grown softer with age and more polished by years of education and practice in appearing humble when it counted. Most notable about Samael were his eyes—one brown, one green. They met Sam's as Samael strode to the middle of the panel before he turned to directly face Gabriel.

Sam had been careful to keep his mind closed during the hearing, mostly out of fear of being even perceived with such arrogance by the panel. But just then he felt the familiar friendly but resolute touch of Camille in his consciousness. She stayed with him long enough to make it clear that she had learned something important from Samael's new form, and then, in her elegant way, was gone. The meaning of her gentle push twisted around and eluded him for a moment. Then his heart jumped. He glanced up at the panel and then quickly away.

"Could you state your name for the Court?" Sam said.

"Samael."

"Also known as?"

"We know all this," Uriel said.

"How long have you been the investigator to God's Council?"

Samael looked across the panel and shrugged slightly. "Time is not as you understand it, Mr. Young. I'm simply not sure how to gauge it for the purposes of your question."

"Just put it into Bible years, Samael, and let's move on with it," Uriel said.

"I've been the Council's investigator for about six thousand years."

"How did you come to be awarded your current position?"

"Objection." Samael's voice was a breathy hiss. "My résumé is irrelevant, Your Honors. You agreed to this hearing to assess the matter concerning Azazel."

Gabriel and Michael exchanged looks again, and Uriel leaned and whispered to Raphael. Gabriel leaned back on his throne, eyes first on Samael and then on Sam. But before Gabriel ruled on the issue, Samael spoke again.

"My position was no award at all." His voice was now calm and resonant. "It was a punishment. A well-deserved punishment

I humbly accepted, and still do."

"You were once a member of the Council, an Angel, and were relegated to your current role as investigator to the Council based on an adjudication, much like this one?"

"Something like that."

"You received this punishment six thousand years ago, you say?"

"About."

"Before God created humans?"

"Yes."

"Before Azazel's transgression?"

"Obviously."

"But after God created the Heavens and the Earth?"

"Of course, yes."

"After God created the Earth, and before you received your punishment, where did you reside?"

"Here and there. Heaven and Earth."

"You were, back then, an Archangel and member of the Council?"

"Yes."

"You heard Azazel testify that between God's creation of Heaven and Earth, and the beginning of life on Earth, eons passed. Do you agree?"

"Yes."

"Are we talking billions of years. Non-Bible years?"

"A half a billion, perhaps, before any life began."

"During which, he further testified, that Earth was a void. Do you agree?"

Samael hesitated. "That seems the accepted narrative."

"For, as you say, half a billion years?"

"About so."

"And by the time humans existed, you had already been, shall we say, stripped of your status as an Archangel in Heaven for several billion years."

"Yes."

"Why were you stripped of your status?"

"Move on," Gabriel said. "I agree with Samael that details of prior matters are irrelevant."

"After the existence of humans began, to what tasks were Azazel and the others assigned?"

"They were assigned by God to watch over Earth. Though it got well beyond watching rather quickly, as we are all regrettably aware."

"Azazel's group of former Angels has been referred to as the Watchers in Scripture, right? Because of their role in watching over the Earth."

"Among other names."

"After the transgression, Azazel and the other Watchers were judged and convicted, in a proceeding much like this one."

"Much like it, yes."

"That is, with this same panel of Angels and you as the Council's investigator. And when you yourself were punished, Azazel was among those bearing witness against you, am I right?"

"Yes," Samael said. "Your Honors, I am beginning to wonder when Mr. Young will ask a question that is relevant to these proceedings."

"We're aware of the judicial history of God's Council, Mr. Young," Uriel said. "You can move on and get to the point, whatever it is. But remember, we also know Samael quite well."

"Your job is not an easy one, is it?" Sam asked Samael. "I mean, your duties require you to spend a fair amount of time on Earth, right?"

"More than a fair amount of work, yes. It's busy. But I don't complain. I deserve what I've gotten.'"

"You meet humans on a regular basis?"

"Meet, not always. Sometimes. It's a bit beyond your understanding."

"Yeah, I imagine your investigative techniques are subtle enough. But you do have human interactions, right?"

"Only when the need is extremely urgent."

"In the Bible, a heavenly being like yourself can interact with people on Earth whether the people know it or not. Is that right?"

"Yes."

"But that doesn't happen much anymore, does it?"

"I'm not sure what you mean."

"For example, Scripture tells us that His Honor Gabriel, His Honor Michael, and Her Honor Raphael have interacted with humans on Earth. When was the last time, to your knowledge, that an Archangel acted on Earth?"

"Not recently," Samael said.

"Except for you."

"I'm not an Archangel."

"When you appear on Earth, what are you like? Man? Woman?"

"It depends. Usually no one pays me any mind. The gift of a good investigator, you know."

"Do you often appear as you are now?"

"I do."

"Do you know a man named Miguel Bilbao?"

"Humans have been around for six million years, Mr. Young. I can't remember everyone."

"Bariloche, Argentina, mid-forties?"

"Not coming to mind."

"He lived with a woman outside town? A shanty town. She had two daughters from a previous relationship? Miguel had a son with her?"

"Not placing it."

"A bit of a drinker? Used to have a friend named Victorio?"

"I am not aware of this."

"You sure, Samael? Miguel and Victorio used to drink together, talk about life, a real simpatico friendship?"

Samael, ashen faced, raised his arms in an unconvincing shrug.

"Miguel was a real friendly guy, generous—you don't remember this? He would let Victorio have sex with his older daughter? That was before Miguel abducted and molested a boy in town? Before his younger daughter killed him? Ringing a bell?"

"Objection," Samael said. "What is the relevance here? I concede that sin exists on Earth. Shall we plod through a trillion examples? It has not been my duty to stop sin."

The panel did not react.

"But I suppose, in fairness, you're not omniscient, right?" Sam said. "You can't be expected to remember everything."

"Of course not."

"After Azazel and the Watchers were bound and cast into the fire under the Earth, who replaced them in their role?"

"I don't understand."

"You've testified that before their transgression, the role of Azazel and his cohorts was to watch over the Earth. The Watchers. After they were sentenced, for seventy generations, who in Heaven took over the role of watching over the Earth?"

"I suppose I never thought much about it," Samael said. "But no one took over."

"No Archangels have been assigned to watch matters on Earth for the last five thousand years?"

"I guess not," Samael said. "Maybe because that didn't work out too well the last time."

"How many investigators to God's Council are there? Other than you?"

"Just me. It's not complicated."

"I thought you said it was busy. 'More than a fair amount of work?'"

"It's a low-status job," Samael said. "Busy, but not too busy for me."

"And what is your job at a meeting of God's Council?"

"To brief the Council about matters on Earth."

"Who calls the meetings?"

"I suppose I do, whenever necessary."

"How often does the Council meet?"

"There are many members on the Council. I'm not made aware of every meeting. Some of them don't include me—so many other things for the members to do than meet with me."

"How often with you? The meetings about matters on Earth?"

"Every so often."

"I'm asking you to state how often, in human years, the Council meets with you."

"There's not a regular schedule, Mr. Young. Mysterious ways, you know. Though you quite plainly do not. I can't say exactly how often."

"Okay. When was the last time the Council met with you about matters on Earth? In days, months, or years."

"Not every meeting is a hearing such as this. If it's God's will, we come calling, without hesitation."

"God's will? I thought you said you call the meetings?"

"When necessary, I do," Samael said. "But if God believes there should be a meeting, of course there is one."

"When was the last one? With you, about matters on Earth?"

Samael glanced across the panel. Receiving no relief, he let the seconds tick by. "The last meeting was about two thousand years ago, give or take."

"Who called that meeting?"

"As I recall, I convened the Council at that time."

"Why?"

Samael hesitated, hoping for an interjection by the panel. None came.

"It concerned His Honor Gabriel, actually," Samael said.

"What about him?"

"I'm allowing evidence of the existence of prior meetings and their timing, but not the details of the prior matters," Gabriel said. "Move on."

"I will, Your Honor. Samael, there was a Council meeting held sometime before that as well," Sam said. "The Book of Job, at 1:6, says:

"One day the Sons of God came to present themselves before God, and Satan also came with them. God said to Satan, 'Where have you come from?'

"Satan answered the LORD, 'From roaming throughout the Earth, going back and forth on it.'

"Then the LORD said to Satan, 'Have you considered my servant, Job? There is no one on Earth like him; he is blameless and upright, a man who fears God and shuns evil.'

"'Does Job fear God for nothing?' Satan replied. 'Have you not provided him riches? You have blessed the work of his hands, so that his flocks and herds are spread throughout the land. But now stretch out your hand and strike down everything he has, and he will surely curse you to your face.'

"Then God said to Satan, 'Very well, then, everything he has is in your power, but on the man himself do not lay a finger.'

"Then Satan went out from the presence of God."

"Are you familiar with this passage, Samael?"

"You recite an English translation, and these, I suppose, stories are never perfectly right."

"But many are not perfectly wrong either. Fair enough?"

"I suppose."

"Do you know of this one?"

"Yes."

"The character in it referred to as Satan—is that you?"

"A translation, as I said," Samael said.

"When was that Council meeting?"

"About twenty-six hundred years ago."

"And after the meeting, you went down to Earth to torment Job to see if you could prove God wrong?"

"That's about right."

"A gentleman's bet?"

"I guess so."

"Which you lost?"

"I did lose that one."

"But again, you're not omniscient. You were only betting that Job's faith would fail, and you turned out to be wrong."

"Exactly."

"As with Jesus?"

"Excuse me?"

"You tempted him. Tested his faith. I'm sure you remember this one quite well. From the Gospel of Luke:

"Then Jesus, being filled with the Holy Spirit, returned from the Jordan and was led by the Spirit into the wilderness, being tempted for forty days by the devil.

"And later:

"And Jesus answered and said to him, 'It has been said, "You shall not tempt the LORD *your God."' Now when the devil had ended every temptation, he departed from Him until an opportune time."*

"You tempted Jesus, too, and he, like Job, passed the test," Sam said.

"An interesting point, Mr. Young," Samael said. "Though Jesus was not a human."

Samael glanced across the panel, resting his eyes on Gabriel.

"A hybrid?" Sam said.

Samael bowed towards the panel, almost, for the first time, as if unsure of how to proceed. "Are we further entertaining the topic of the origins of Jesus of Nazareth?"

"Let's move on,'" Gabriel said.

"Would it be fair to say that you enjoy intrigue, Samael?" Sam said.

"I'm not sure what you mean."

"Drama. Dalliance. Betrayal. You know what I mean. Complexity."

"Humans adore such things, Mr. Young. It's their nature. I did not create them, did I?"

"When, Samael, was the last time you proposed a meeting of God's Council before the one concerning His Honor Gabriel?"

Samael hesitated again, glancing sideways at Gabriel, who remained impassive. "It was about five thousand years ago, give or take."

"What was the subject of that meeting?" Sam said.

"Azazel and the transgressors."

"Am I right," Sam said, "that in six thousand years, as the investigator for God's Council tasked with reporting on problems on Earth, you've requested only two meetings with the Council?"

"I think that's right."

"One, concerning His Honor Gabriel, and the other, in which you argued that the Watchers be imprisoned under the Earth for seventy generations?"

"Yes," Samael said. "Your Honors, are we quite through?"

"Samael, I have one last area of inquiry. You are aware that hybrids, the offspring of Angels and humans, exist on Earth."

"Yes, though very few, as far as I know."

"You were aware of that before this hearing?"

"Yes."

"You've met at least one of them, haven't you?"

"No."

"A hybrid is not a human, you would agree?"

"Yes, by definition that would be so."

"So, an Angel—sorry, a personage—from Heaven, having sex with a hybrid would not necessarily violate God's law—at least not the law you used to accuse the Watchers."

"I agree with that. Certainly not that law. Perhaps it's a gray area."

"You've been banking on it being a gray area, haven't you? For many years now."

"I don't understand."

"If you never knew Miguel Bilbao and his teenage daughters, then how did you know that Trinity and Fifika were, in your words, sexually abused by a demented man and his friends?"

"Your Honors, this has gone on long enough," Samael said. "I object."

"Miguel Bilbao was an easy target, wasn't he? Not quite so resilient as Job? How much did he charge you?"

"This is irrelevant."

"But most humans are pretty weak, right, Victorio?"

"That's not my fault."

"How old was Trinity Kritalsh when Miguel let you tend to her? Fifteen?"

"This inquiry is a waste of the Council's time," Samael said.

"She was a hybrid, not a human, so no violation, right?"

Samael did not reply.

"But it's the humans who love intrigue, right?" Sam said.

"Your Honors should put a stop to this line of questioning," Samael said.

"You claim neither Azazel and the Watchers, nor their children, deserve relief," Sam said. "Yet you seek to bar the Council from consideration of your own behavior or that of other members of the Heavenly Host?"

"I have sought to bar nothing of the sort. The panel has

excluded the matter of the origins of Jesus, I see no reason this topic should be any different, and—"

"Enough," Gabriel said. Uriel hunched on his throne, shaking his head. Michael's eyes blazed. "This hearing is over. We will retire to discuss the matter before considering brief arguments."

The thrones eased away. They became hills, and then mountains in the distance. Samael, once again a beautiful young woman with gleaming black eyes, turned slowly to look at Sam. They flashed, and the panel had returned.

CHAPTER
TWENTY-EIGHT

"IT SEEMS TO ME," Gabriel said, "that there are four ways this can be. One, we do nothing. I, for one, believe that option to be cruel. These hybrids, with all their flaws, have no fault in their own creation and suffer enormously when they grow old. Certainly, suffering is part of life on Earth, but to condemn an entire class to preordained misery is not something we've done before.

"Two, we grant the petition as to the hybrids and deny the petition with respect to Azazel and the other transgressors. But even that doesn't solve the problem, because the transgressors won't stop creating new hybrids if left on Earth.

"The third option is to grant the petition for the hybrids and to bind Azazel and the others back in the fire to stop them from creating more hybrids.

"Finally, we could grant the petition for both classes. I wish to hear my colleagues' opinions on these options. First, we will hear a brief statement from both of you, Mr. Young and Samael. Mr. Young?"

"Excuse me, Your Honor, Gabriel," Sam said. "If I may, how is the decision reached. By a vote?"

"A fair question. Our rulings are always unanimous."

"Esteemed Court, the noncanonical Book of Enoch details Azazel's role in the transgression that has been the subject of this hearing. He was one of the Watchers, a group of Angels tasked with watching over the Earth. But the name Azazel appears again, in exactly one passage, in the canonical Hebrew Bible. It's in the Book of Leviticus, verse 16: 6-10, where God instructs Moses on how his brother Aaron, the high priest of the Israelites, should approach God in the Most Holy Place on the annual Day of Atonement—the first Yom Kippur. Leviticus tells us, 'Aaron is to offer a bull for his own sin offering to make atonement for himself and his household. Then he shall take the two goats and set them before the Lord at the entrance of the tent of meeting. And Aaron shall cast lots over the two goats, one lot for the Lord and the other lot for Azazel. And Aaron shall present the goat on which the lot fell for the Lord and use it as a sin offering, but the goat on which the lot fell for Azazel shall be presented alive before the Lord to make atonement over it, that it may be sent away into the wilderness to Azazel.'

"As we know from the facts adduced at this trial, Azazel, by the time of Leviticus, had long since been bound under the Earth on an order from this Council and bore no responsibility for tempting the Israelites, or anyone else alive on Earth at that time, into sin. Yet God instructed Aaron to sacrifice one goat to God as an offering, and to leave the second goat alive to carry the sins of all the Israelites to Azazel. Hence the Day of Atonement—the Israelites' sins were stripped from them and transferred to a goat and then to Azazel. A scapegoat. That's where we get this word. A scapegoat is a person who is blamed for the wrongdoings, faults, or mistakes of others, often for reasons of expediency. Today Samael seeks to use Azazel as a scapegoat once again. Not to take away human sins, but his own and, respectfully, yours."

Sam paused for a moment and glanced out the windows rather than into the eyes of the council. A featureless desert stretched away toward a distant horizon. "These old stories are all from a time, long since passed, when Heaven took part in the world. I'm asking you to take part again, now, to right the wrongs against the claimants in both classes. Our remedies are warranted today because today is the Day of Atonement. The anniversary of the scapegoating of Azazel. Yom Kippur."

"Finally, it must be said that denial of the petition would create a dramatic unwarranted disparity with this court's prior decisions in that the birth of Jesus of Nazareth—"

Gabriel extended his palm towards Sam, but said nothing for a long moment except to lean back and whisper something to Michael.

"Is that right, Samael?" Raphael said. "Today is Yom Kippur?"

Samael remained in her seat. "It is."

"We've heard enough, Mr. Young," Gabriel said. "Argument, Samael?"

Samael stood, bowing slightly to the panel, a gesture that seemed graceful and substantial now in her female form. "Nothing for me to add. I leave the matter to your wise discretion."

Gabriel looked to Sarakiel.

"To put it bluntly, we've tried to wipe out the hybrids several times," Sarakiel said. "The flood. The battle for Canaan. Jericho. We obviously failed, as Samael has conceded. If we don't grant the petition as to the hybrids, it'll just be more trouble. I think Samael enjoys the idea of humans learning, on a large scale, about the existence of the hybrids, which they will if this man in Virginia is executed while still a hybrid. But Samael very much enjoys, as Mr. Young says, intrigue. As we well learned at our last trial concerning the allegations—and, to be clear, unproven allegations—against Gabriel. Today, Samael declines to point out the unproven nature of that allegation even though the analogy would aid her cause. I would grant the petition as to class two. As for the Watchers, I defer to the group."

"I personally bound and buried Azazel last time around," Raphael said. "I felt conflicted about it, but orders are orders, and he appears not to have learned his lesson. However—" Raphael took off his glasses. "Azazel, you did serve your sentence, and it was a long one. And I do think we have to consider the motives of the parties before us. Mr. Young and the class one and two claimants are asking for forgiveness. An understandable motive, which derives from the main characteristic of all creatures on Earth—selfishness. But Samael, by seeking denial of both claims, wishes the transgressors to remain on Earth, thereby creating more hybrids, who will then live again and again until they go mad. We'll wind up with the very same problem we had before we bound Azazel in the first place. I defer to the group."

"A rather flawed analysis," Uriel said. He smiled broadly, hands on his gut, sandals stretched out in front of him. "I've always believed we should deny both claims. That processes on Earth always play out as they should, which is the will of God—let's not forget that. Samael keeps things moving along on Earth and reports back, and I agree we could tighten up that arrangement a bit, but Mr. Young's suit asks us to change the biology of these creatures. God's creatures. Evolution on Earth has done so, but we never have." Uriel paused. "Yet this matter has delved into long resolved issues best left in the past. In the interest of moving forward, and out of my respect for brother Gabriel, I defer to the group on both decisions. Day of Atonement, I suppose." He glanced at Gabriel.

"I believe the immortal nature of the hybrids was an unintended consequence," Raguel said. "Not even Azazel and the transgressors intended it, least of all God. Of course, that's the problem with what the transgressors did in the first place, which we all know God also never intended. I submit that it is God's intentions that control the issue, and those intentions which distinguish the case concerning Gabriel from this one. It has never been God's will to intervene to prevent a species from becoming extinct, or a person or class of persons from dying, but God did seek to wipe out the hybrids at least once before, though apparently it didn't work out that way. Wouldn't granting the petition as to class two be, in effect, wiping them out? As it stands now, they will never become extinct as all other creatures do, and should. That is God's will. I say we grant the petition as to both classes."

"Azazel was a loyal soldier in the war," Michael said, glancing down at Azazel. His hand still rested on his sword. "He's been punished. I would grant the petition as to both classes."

The entire panel looked to Gabriel.

"It shall be the ruling of God's Council that the hybrids on Earth from the original Fall, and those born after the release of the Watchers, shall remain hybrids, as the natural processes have dictated, until such time as each individual chooses to become human, and thus dies in his natural course."

Gabriel hesitated just then, turning towards Samael, who sat straight, even defiant with her pursed lips and narrowed eyes. "This Council shall reconvene forthwith to decide what, if anything, should be done about any potential negligent if not intentional mismanagement of Earth that has occurred since the Fall of the Watchers. Samael shall be present. A new panel will be formed to adjudicate the matter."

Gabriel now regarded Azazel. He then leaned forward, glaring at Samael again, who now stood. Gabriel, whose chosen visage had been one of a clichéd older gentleman, an outdated archetype of a judge, CEO, or president, was now an androgynous spirit in flesh form, as depicted in a piece of revered wordly art.

"Samael, you have continually tried to infuse this trial with an unseemly and dishonest point," Gabriel said. "This court will not be re-adjudicating the scandalous charge you brought against me two thousand years ago, a charge based on your skewed understanding of my mission to Mary of Nazareth."

The members of the court focused with rapt attention on Gabriel. Even Raguel had dispensed with admiring her manicure to give full heed to the chief judge.

"Let me, however briefly, refresh Samael's poor memory of that long-ago trial. I was declared innocent of being, how shall I say it, sexually involved in the conception of Mary's son. Yes, I came to her. I also departed from her, as explained in Luke 1:38, and I delivered my Lord God's message to her and nothing more, despite unfortunate translations and gossip suggesting otherwise. Now, let's return to the matter at hand."

But Sarakiel, perhaps having noticed with some amount of glee that Samael was declining to make eye contact with the chief judge, leaned towards Gabriel. "With your Honor Gabriel's permission, I would like to offer a few comments before we move on."

"Are they relevant, Sarakiel?" Gabriel said.

"They could be, my dear Gabriel."

"Briefly please. And Sarakiel, you will not be offering esoteric commentary on the so-called Virgin Birth, one of your favorite musings."

"Certainly not. This is not the opportune time for such a discussion. My two comments are more mundane. Point number one: Like all members of the court, I never questioned the truth-seeking motivation behind our investigator's passion in bringing that long-ago accusation against our esteemed colleague Gabriel. Why? Because Mary of Nazareth, like the women chosen by Azazel and the others many years before, conceived under suspicious circumstances, that is, without intercourse with a human. But also because it became apparent during that trial that

Samael's accusation, which appeared reasonable at first glance, was based upon her fundamentally inept grasp of the nuances of Luke's Greek text, regarding both individual words and those in-between verses. Don't get me started on Samael's so-called facility with Aramaic and Hebrew. Back then, this panel attributed Samael's failure to discern the truth about Gabriel's mission to his inability to struggle with Luke's somewhat highbrow Greek."

Sarakiel paused for a moment, almost as if daring Samael to butt in. "Point two: Now I'm not so sure. As we set the matter straight so long ago, Samael's continual belaboring of the point makes me consider the more disturbing motive of vendetta, be it against Azazel or indeed Gabriel himself, both of whom played roles in his fall from Archangel status long before life on Earth even began, let alone human or hybrid life. That is all, Gabriel. Thank you."

"I'd like to make a brief addendum to your eloquent rendition of events, Your Honors," Samael said. "Mary of Nazareth was a human, not a hybrid. Similarly, one of Azazel's Watchers must have transgressed with a human woman after his release, spawning Cinderella Baptista at least."

"Or did someone else father Baptista?" Sam said. "Maybe a heavenly personage who regularly visits the world? Who believes him or herself unmonitored by the Council? Maybe Samael hopes it's been a while, in her words, since anyone cared. And Baptista was just a gypsy, right? Not exactly the chosen people, are they, Samael?"

"Objection," Samael said. "There has been no evidence presented to suggest my involvement in anything to do with Cinderella Baptista."

"Whatever happened, you likely know of it, Samael," Gabriel said. "And I note it was not you who convened today's Council, was it?"

Samael folded her arms and stared at the ground for a long moment, then her eyes darted to Sam, catching him by surprise such that he recognized, just before she began to speak, the crystallizing within her of an of an accord. If only with herself.

"Your Honor Gabriel," Samael said. "I was demoted to the Council's Investigator long ago as a punishment, and I've gently accepted the burden so that this esteemed Council and your colleagues—indeed, even He—need not trouble with Earth so much as before. Quite frankly, I've believed you had rather gotten over it. And it's not as if I've been hiding. Your Honor Sarakiel, when did you last discuss humans with the Great One or his son? And you, Raphael, have you engaged with that part of creation since you bound up Azazel 'way back when? Your Honor Michael, I know you're a great warrior, but whom have you fought lately? And Raguel, said to be the Archangel of justice, fairness, and harmony, what do you know of those topics on Earth these near two thousand years since the Place of Skulls? Uriel, Archangel of punishment and salvation, can you honestly say you've performed both of those rules in recent memory? Or just one of them? The one you enjoy most, perhaps? And if anything was made clear to me at our last hearing, it was that Jesus—wherever he came from, dear Gabriel—has sovereignty over the souls of humans, over me, and, yes, even over you. And yet, for ever so long . . . nothing. Your Honors, I object to any innuendo that I've done anything but my duty."

Gabriel, an old man again, made eye contact with Sam. "Mr. Young, your petition as to Azazel and the Watchers is also granted. And Samael?"

"Yes, Your Honor Gabriel?"

"We'll see you back here soon."

• • •

Sam shivered. The breeze on Mount Hermon seemed colder than before. He glanced at his phone. *12:58.*

"So be it, I suppose." Samael said. "How'd you do that?"

"Do what?"

"Keep Gabriel out of your head—about Jesus? About the old allegation concerning the so-called virgin? You fucked with him, Samson. And he blamed it on me,. Well played. I found it rather delicious."

"I'm not sure what you're talking about."

"Oh, but you are. In any case, I hope to see you soon."

"Why?" Sam asked.

"When you defend me at my trial," Samael said. "What do they call it? The Nuremberg defense? Just following orders, right? Or maybe it's as simple as the fact that no one ever set rules for me in the first place. I was never tasked with looking after the children of Azazel, to say nothing of humans. Nor has such looking-after been the will of any god I've known. Me, negligent? If any heavenly personage should be tried for betraying those on Earth, it's Jesus for his lofty promises. Maybe along with Gabriel and that do-nothing Council. What a case that would be." Samael spoke softly, but with an edge in her voice as if, for the first time, she felt a real passion for one of her points.

Sam watched his friends, who stood in a row gazing over the ridge into Syria. Van Zyl was not among them.

"If you think this case paid well," Samael said, "you have no idea what defending me could bring. You like causes, don't you? You and the Kritalsh girls love your causes. We can work together, Samson. Set things right."

"Have we met before?" Sam said. "On Earth?"

Samael laughed and turned away, gazing across the snow in the opposite direction from the group.

"Whatever you decide, you'd also make a fine investigator to God's Council someday." Samael smiled, as beautiful as before, and extended her hand. Sam took it. "Until the opportune time, I suppose."

Samael walked away across the snow, and Sam watched her until she disappeared down the far side of the ridge.

"Hey, Young!" They all turned towards the way they had come to see O'Donald trudging up the hill. "Time's up. Colonel says to bring you down."

"Colonel Guy's gonna notice we lost someone up here, Bubba," Nguyen said to Sam. "He's gonna violate our no-fly zones."

Sam, Amelia, and Nguyen followed the others across the snow towards the Irishman, who waved his blue beret wildly over his head.

"No," Sam said. "He's really not."

CHAPTER
TWENTY-NINE

TWO WEEKS LATER, 7:50 A.M.

Sam parked the Escalade in one of the angled spots immediately in front of his office. His phone buzzed.

"Hey, William."

"You ready for court?"

"Yep."

"You have what you need?"

"The profile developed from the swab I sent you last week is not the genetic profile of Igor Alexi. DFS obviously made a mistake with their original testing. Igor's actual profile is not homozygotic at any loci. It's a normal profile. It shares one allele at every locus with the light switch flipper, and with the original Department of Forensic Science profile purporting to be Igor's. But this profile cannot be the light switch flipper's or the previous Igor Alexi profile. The judge is gonna have to order new testing through the state lab."

"Does the judge have to let him withdraw his guilty plea?"

"Doesn't have to, but he will. We have proof the DNA evidence in the case was wrong. Judge Chan hates criminals. But he loves the law."

"Which means no DNA in the case. But didn't Igor confess?" William said. "At the new trial, can they just use that?"

"That's the funny part," Sam said. "They won't be able to use the in-court confession he made at his guilty plea if the plea gets withdrawn. Which leaves his confession to Vick. But Vick's gone."

"What do you mean, gone?"

"They can't find him. He split. He's on the run."

"I didn't know anyone did that anymore. Can he actually get away?"

"If anyone can, he can," Sam said. "And he's recently had a cash infusion. More importantly, what are you two doing next week? I'm taking Alifair to Disneyworld. Want to join?"

"Since when do you have time for a vacation?" William asked.

"Ha. I recently earned a rather large fee in a quirky case. It's kind of under seal, but you may have heard of it."

"Do tell," William said. "So Young and Griffin is folding up?"

"Of course not. Upgrading. I'm just getting good at this shit."

"One more thing," William said. "I anonymously uploaded the Lugnudsky profile into the Genematch database. Do you want to know how many potential relatives we found?"

Sam, walking towards Starbucks, glanced at the time on his phone. *8:20.* "Right now, I really don't. I'll send you guys the info on Orlando." He hung up.

"Back from vacation, Bubba?"

Sam turned towards the voice. "Hey, there."

"I think you owe me a coffee," Tawana said. "It took me hours to get that radiator out of the floor, and Naser charged me for breaking the dang thing. The bastard also sent me a cleaning bill to get all that crusty-ass blood out of the carpet."

"You were gonna kill me that day."

"Yeah."

"Well, I'm glad you didn't."

"Hey, have you seen this?" Tawana held her phone up to Sam. He took the phone and expanded the screen. A local newspaper from down south. *The Abingdon Virginian*. The headline read, *John Williamson, 1925-2019*. Esau's selfie, cropped to depict only his face, loomed next to the brief obituary.

"Good for him, I say," Tawana said. "But if you try to collect my empty coffee cup for some of your scientific foolishness, I'm gonna grind your beans, Bubba. I'm immortal. Feels good, huh?"

Sam followed her into the store. "It does feel good. At least for now."

"I did wanna see you though," she said.

He nodded. "I know. People should stay with their kind."

EPILOGUE

The young woman shopped slowly, examining various items—shirts, hats, local crafts, books, maps, colorful woven pullovers, assorted outdoor gear—until she found precisely those she needed. She could not buy much. She had plenty of cash, but whatever she bought would have to fit on her person. She knew that no matter how she dressed or what she carried, the old fortuneteller would immediately peg her for an American, but she did not need the other residents of the Stolipinovo ghetto seeing her toting a bag from a local gift store.

She was tired but excited and, yes, scared. After many ups and downs, her journey, which had taken her from Washington, DC, to Havana to Argentina to Sofia and, today, to the touristy section of Plovdiv, Bulgaria, was nearly complete. One more trek down the highway, away from the restaurants and stores and the ancient Roman coliseum up the hill, and she would rest. Her guidebook said not to miss the coliseum. A rare chance to explore an ancient treasure from the second century CE. But she had not bothered to stroll up the hill to experience it. She explored a much older mystery.

"Cash?"

"Cash," she said to the Bulgarian kid at the register, glancing at the bills in her extended hand as she said it. The cashier watched her with seeming curiosity as he packaged the serrated camping knife in a small cloth bag.

She put on her new glasses, stowed her fancy knife in the side pocket of her cargo pants, and eased out of the shop and onto the street, where the sun beamed down on the tourists hustling to lunch or maybe to do more shopping. She also repocketed the crisp lev the clerk had declined to request. Instead of asking her to hand over the bills, he had only smiled at her, almost as if to wink. Almost as if he were in on it.

She didn't like to steal. But sometimes it was hard to resist. Her cousin always told her not to be frivolous with her gift, but she eyed him skeptically whenever he issued that advice. He always smiled and turned away.

She chose a side street off the main Plovdiv strip. She looked at her boots as she walked but paid attention to everything around her all the same. She had about two miles to go, and then maybe nowhere for a while. Her cousin liked to tell her that if she stayed quiet, "slowed down time," as he put it, she would be able to see the meanings and origins of things. She breathed deeply and slowly as she walked. *Slow time. Observe.*

It would be easy to tell the difference between a Bulgarian and a Roma. But between a Roma from the west and a Gypsy born and raised in the Stolipinovo ghetto? She was not so sure. But she supposed they would come to know each other quickly enough if her quest turned out to be successful. And if not, she had always been pretty fast on her feet. And now she had the knife.

She walked quickly along the side of the highway that led out of town and could soon see the blocky, Soviet-era structures. Why so many satellite dishes? The buildings looked pretty from afar, the multicolored laundry drying on the balconies seemed to hint that a Disney village filled with old stories and dancing would appear around the bend.

Twenty minutes later, she stood still and her mind reached as far and strenuously as it could—up, down, and around the buildings and through the alleys shooting off the main ghetto thoroughfare, the sewer pit down the middle like a pitiable and accidental mimicry of Venice's Grand Canal. The foothills of trash piled against the buildings on either side of the street—also artistic, with their patterns of blue, green, and red broken up by gray—belonged in this picture too.

Where are you?

She recalled her cousin's eulogy at her mother's funeral last year. "What a life!" he had said. But the expression seemed like an inside joke, as many things had between those two.

A dog's barking at her broke her concentration. It came no closer than a few feet, granting her the space to continue straight on by if she wished. A sentry? A warning from beyond? Maybe just a hungry mutt with tight skin. Her cousin told her years ago that a grouchy dog in their neighborhood barked so much because her old skin was too tight. Her cousin always floated strange ideas and closely observed her responses. Even as a girl, she knew it wasn't true, but the image of the tight-skinned dog remained. This dog seemed to say the same thing again and again. *Ruff, ruff, ruff.* Always in threes. Did he issue a warning? A welcome?

She guessed it was about eleven in the morning but stopped herself from launching her band to check the time. *Do not go into the Stolipinovo ghetto as a tourist,* a guidebook said. *Many people are robbed and assaulted every year.*

She cast her eyes down at her boots. *Slow time. Observe.*

She carried the old journal in the other pocket of her cargo pants. A new knife and some old family lore. Perfect gear for her kind—a Gypsy from far away.

But we're not people.

She strode alongside the open sewer, her mind trolling, to and fro down the offshoots and alleys. *Are you really here?*

She knew how to troll for auras. And she knew the one for which she searched would feel something like her mother's, but different, too. Stronger. Perhaps more magical. Her mother's aura had waned as she got older and, when she died, had felt merely like most of them do. Unique, but muted by the noise of the world.

The residents of Stolipinovo appeared to pose no threat to her, just a few glances and whispers between small groups of adults. A few young children followed her, indeed, practically skipped along behind her. The place simply felt old, and not just because of the dilapidated Soviet buildings. The feeling flowed as much, or more, from the soft, tired emotions emanating from the narrow alleys and open windows. People did watch from above but seemed to view her as a typical foreign interloper—not too exciting, at least not on the ghetto's main thoroughfare in the bright light of day.

She glanced down one alley and then another as she strode, hands by her side, until an opening between the buildings to her left drew her attention. When she approached, at an angle that allowed her a view down the narrow passage, she saw a boy, maybe ten years old, beckoning her. He waved towards her with both hands, eyes excited. But of course, she had read about this before. Children decoying tourists towards a rip-off or a robbery. The boy was, however, not a burgeoning con artist, at least not right then.

The feeling hit her as she stepped into the alley towards the boy. There was a warmth, like immersion in water of the perfect temperature, and the soft smell of fresh fruit, maybe a mix of oranges and limes blended for a fancy lotion.

"Come, come, come," the boy said. He had a little dog with him, like a beagle but with stumpier legs. The dog followed him into a doorway and then turned and yelped at her, friendly compared to the harsher barks of the old dog by the highway. Mixed messages from the ghetto, she supposed. *People should stay with their kind*

She peered into the doorway and the boy was halfway up the stairs, which seemed part of a common access to apartments and had a low ceiling and barely enough room between the walls for two to walk up abreast. The boy, dog at his heel, motioned again. She followed, up one flight and then twisting back to another until the three of them entered single file through the open door of an apartment. The warmth was here too, and the aroma, but stronger.

"Hello, Alifair."

Alifair turned quickly to see a middle-aged woman sitting on a wooden chair by an open window. An ancient gypsy man sitting on the other side of the window held a cup of what may have been the orange-lime tea. His skin was wrinkled like none she had ever seen.

"Hello, Aunt Fifika." Alifair touched her pocket, feeling the journal.

"I'm sorry to hear about your, mom," Fifika said. "But what a life."

The stumpy-legged dog barked again, and again, and again.

CPSIA information can be obtained
at www.ICGtesting.com
Printed in the USA
LVHW091353310321
683079LV00019B/172